Lather Rinse Repeat

Lather Rinse Repeat

stories

David Tabak

Aquitaine

Copyright 2012 David Tabak.
All rights reserved.

ISBN 978-0-9846965-1-2

Cover detail from Andy Finkle, *Mensa (Sad Egghead)* (2008).

All interior illustrations by Andy Finkle, and used with the gracious permission of the artist. See www.andyfinkle.com for more information.

Cover and titles are set in Nebish Serif, created by Andy Finkle.

Catalog-in-Publication Data:
    Tabak, David (1965-)
    Lather rinse repeat: stories, David Tabak.
    Chicago: Aquitaine Media, 2012.
    220 pp, pbk.
    Adult: Fiction: United States
    Short stories: United States: Fiction
    Jews: United States: Fiction
    Short stories: Jewish
    Dewey class.: 813.54.222

Aquitaine Media Corp., Chicago IL   www.aquitainebooks.com

For Denise,
who has always been content to get lost with me

Contents

Ginsberg the Swede	1
Mulligan	19
The Bruegel Birthday Kompany	33
The Naked Sniper	49
A Stone's Throw	75
I'm With Stupid	91
Veal	103
Straight and Narrow	117
Half Off Until Nine	135
Five People, Not Including the Guy with the Broom	147
Alice and Angus	165
Caring	183
Waiting	199

Ginsberg the Swede

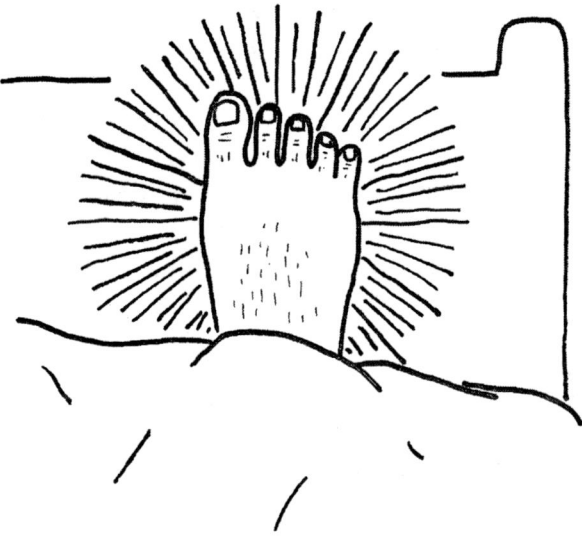

On Tuesday morning, Ginsberg awoke in another man's body. He had slept unusually well the night before. He had not been kept awake by the usual worries or migraines and awoke completely refreshed for the first time in his life.

Stretching contently, he noticed he had grown taller during the night, too. Even with his head against the headboard, his legs were slightly bent, with his feet flat against the footboard. And what feet they were! Strong, well-formed feet with straight toes and pink, healthy toenails. These were clearly not his feet as they were at least three sizes larger. Questions flitted about Ginsberg's brain like a feather falling on a spring morning: "Whose feet are they and what are they doing in my bed?"

Ginsberg began to move the alien feet about. He imagined squeezing the long toes into a ball and squealed with delight when they obeyed. He banged them together, applauding. He never realized feet could be so much fun.

He spent thirty-eight years with yellow, crusty nails on misshapen toes attached to feet so small that he usually shopped in the children's department for a better selection. Most of his shoes had some sort of animal on the soles.

The first thing Ginsberg did each morning was reach for a pair of dark socks that he had strategically placed at the foot of the bed the night before. He tried to look at his feet as little as possible. But not today. These feet wouldn't fit into his socks and it seemed a shame to hide them.

Ginsberg looked at the feet again. They were nearly a perfect peach hue and whoever previously possessed them had taken meticulous care of them. Ginsberg brought the soles of the feet together and noticed no roughness or bone out of place. These were beautiful feet.

Whose feet were they? He thought about all the people he met yesterday. Certainly none of his customers had such feet. They were all in the soft drink business and not one of them had missed the opportunity to drop a keg on their feet. These feet had never felt so much as a splinter.

He thought about whom he had seen at the gym last night. Ginsberg went infrequently due to the sheer uselessness of the effort. But last night he was nervous about today's presentation to the gentlemen from South America that he went to the gym to work off the tension. He rode an exercise bike at the lowest level.

The gym was populated by people much better looking and agile than him. They climbed the Stairmaster at the highest level. They glistened while he melted on the bike's handlebars. Everything seemed easy for these people and he was sure these feet belonged to someone from the gym. But who?

He looked at the feet again and calculated the person must be well over six feet tall. They had the slightest hint of downy har on the knuckles. A blonde!

Now he knew whose feet these were: the Swede's. Ginsberg did not know for a fact that the man was Swedish. They never spoke, even when they were alone in the elevator. Men like the Swede didn't talk to men like Ginsberg.

Ginsberg called him the Swede because of his body was nearly perfect. His wavy blonde hair was thick and luxurious and could only be the result of a proper Lutheran upbringing. Ginsberg smiled when he considered the confusion the Swede must be experiencing at that moment when he awoke to find himself with gnarled, hairy, stubby Jew feet. They shared the same confusion, but the Swede had the extra benefit of revulsion.

To alleviate his guilt, Ginsberg reminded himself that, since he did not know the Swede's name, there was no way of contacting him to exchange feet. Ginsberg tried not to smile too broadly. Besides, who could begrudge him nice feet for a change? The rest of the Swede was nearly perfect. Or was it?

Ginsberg began to pull off the covers, performing a reverse striptease. The shins were obviously the Swede's as well and the knees were gorgeous. They were well-proportioned and parallel. Ginsberg imagined the Swede's confusion as he tried to figure his new knees' affinity for each other.

Ginsberg looked his hands. If they had not been smooth and well-manicured, he would have sworn that they were worker's hands. They were large and substantially constructed. What fascinated Ginsberg the most was the long slender fingers pointing in the same direction. They were very much unlike his own hands, which resembled nothing so much as knotted, furry claws.

By this time the Swede must be thinking he was the victim of an experiment gone horribly awry. If Ginsberg hadn't discovered the muscular thighs next, he would have actually pitied the Swede, who he was sure was crying by now.

He decided to delay examining the penis that was encased in his briefs, saving that treat for dessert. But curiosity got the better of him and a quick examination found it to be substantial though flaccid and thankfully circumcised.

He felt his stomach; instead of finding a distended liver, which gave him the appearance of being perpetually three months pregnant, he found only hard rigid muscles, neatly lined up in a row.

His chest was impressive and wide. He held his arms straight in front of him and noticed no abnormalities except for the fact that his biceps were prodigious. Ginsberg didn't know what to do with his attraction for his new body.

My God, he thought relishing the ability to move the bed simply by flexing his feet, this is wonderful, simply wonderful. But suddenly he sat upright with speed that startled him. What about his face?

He imagined the Swede, as fate's surrogate, laughing at him. It was a horrific sight to see this large, well-formed handsome head atop Ginsberg's misshapen body; the Swede's blond hair in stark contrast to the hairy torso. He resembled nothing so much as a yin-yang symbol.

If the Swede still had his head, what did Ginsberg have on top of his broad shoulders? He had to know. If his fears were realized, could he exchange the face for the body? Ginsberg had always wanted to be just another pretty face.

Ginsberg lay in bed, ignoring the small round mirror on the top of his bureau. Mornings, he would see a dark shadow floating ominously in front of his face. When he put on his thick glasses, the shadow would resolve itself into his dark troubled face, perpetually in need of a shave.

But wait a minute! He realized everything in the room was clear. Feeling for his glasses, he gratefully poked himself in the eye. He swiveled and saw them on the nightstand, soap-stained from wearing them in the shower.

He looked further to the right and directly at the mirror on top of the bureau; the Swede's face stared back at him angrily. His eyebrows were knit closely as if he were considering placing charges against Ginsberg for theft. Ginsberg averted his eyes by habit and only after he took three deep breaths did he look back into the mirror. This time the Swede regarded Ginsberg with a puzzled look.

Poor Swede. Ginsburg had long ago accepted the fact that his body and face were nothing to write home about and although he was sure that time would take its toll, there was very little further damage that could be done. More of the same, he figured.

But the Swede. All he could expect was a giant fall from grace. A faint, perhaps toothless, smile replacing what used to be. Ginsberg reached up and stroked the Swede's face in sympathy. When he realized he felt both the Swede's firm features and the strong fingers working their way across his face, the Swede in the mirror smiled and laughed. All sympathy for the Swede fell away like a passing cloud. My God, he thought, I'm gorgeous. He threw his head back into pillow and it landed with a definite thud as if it contained new deep thoughts.

Ginsberg's revelry was disturbed by a sudden knock on the door. The knocking had all the hallmarks of his mother, simultaneously apologetic and insistent. It must be late. His mother would not dare to wake him up unless the house was on fire. Usually, she would sit downstairs, gnawing her lower lip in worry and hoping Ginsberg would be awakened by her mouse-like activities in the kitchen.

What time was it? He looked over at the clock. It was 7:15! He should be out the door by now! There was no way he could be at his desk by 8:00 and by 8:05 he was sure that his boss would call. "Oh no reason," Mr. Taxin would say, "I just wanted make sure he will be into work. I figured there must be some reason he's not in today. Today of all days. Why today? Didn't he tell you? Why, Mrs. Ginsberg, your son is on the verge of landing the largest deal in the history of the company. The South America account," he said in reverential tone. "I know. That's why I figured that maybe your son is sick or was hit by a bus. He's still sleeping? You have to excuse me for laughing. You see it is just too ludicrous to believe. I mean a man could lose his job over something like this. Are you sure he's sleeping? Maybe he died. Oh, I know, God forbid, but there has to be a reason. A man doesn't sleep when an opportunity to dominate an entire continent's soft drink industry knocks."

The banging on the door became louder. "Just a minute, please," Ginsberg shouted to the back of the door. "Yes, Mama, I'm up." He looked over at the mirror and whispered, "And I'm beautiful." But there was no time for fantasies now. He had to get to work and explain why he was late. He hoped his transformation would be excuse enough, but couldn't risk being any later than he already was.

The sound his feet made hitting the ground surprised him. Not only were they more substantial than his prior feet, they landed sooner than expected. That's right, I'm taller, he thought. It never dawned on him that he might have difficulty operating his new body.

Great, he had his dream body, but he didn't have the instruction manual. He wasn't sure he could even stand up. Why today of all days? Being in the carbonation business was tenuous at best, and now he could see all the bubbles that this opportunity represented bursting in the air. He didn't appreciate the irony that his career would be ruined because all his fantasies had been fulfilled.

But gradually, like a butterfly (yes, just like a butterfly, Ginsberg thought) emerging from its cocoon, Ginsberg adjusted to his new body. At first his movements were painfully tentative. Everything in his room seemed to be nine inches closer. He would reach out for an item (say the mirror on the dresser) and it would appear in his hands sooner than he expected. His walk to the closet door took half the time it took yesterday.

Ginsberg believed his life was the way it was because he was always late. Teams had been chosen before he arrived at the playground. Celebrities were spotted and gone before he rounded the corner. He had never quite met the woman of his dreams, who he was sure had just left. But now as he set speed records across his room, he understood why. His legs had been too short.

The pounding on the door disturbed his discovery. "I'm coming, Mama." His firm fist gripped the puny doorknob. The door was open before he realized he should explain the wondrous changes that occurred during the night. "Mama, wait..."

Ginsberg started, but stopped when he was faced with a vision of his mother suddenly thirty years younger. Had the whole family been transformed?

It was not his mother who stood slack-jawed in front of him, but Ginsberg's younger sister, Rachel, who had been sent to wake him. Her hair was still half in curlers and she was wearing a white blouse, no pants, and fuzzy pink slippers.

"Hello," was all she could manage. She squeezed the bottom of her blouse together and swayed her hips slightly. Was she embarrassed or aroused?

"Rachel," he said, "it's me." His voice belonged to someone else with a slight rasp to it. "Do I smoke?" Ginsberg wondered. Cigarettes irritated his asthma. When speaking on the phone he had to say "Mister Ginsberg" when someone asked if he went by Miss or Mrs. But now he had the type of voice that could tell the most pathetic joke and have the whole room laughing if for no other reason to get on his good side.

For some reason Rachel didn't question who Ginsberg meant by "me." It could have been she was in shock or the fact he was not wearing a shirt and she was trying not to stare at his broad chest. It was the first time Rachel hadn't told him "for God's sake, put on a shirt, your breasts are bigger than mine!" Today, brother and sister shared a rare familiar moment of intimacy as they admired his new body.

"Rachel," their mother called from the base of the stairs, "is he up? Rachel, did you hear me? Is he up? Rachel, why don't you answer me?"

Rachel's eyes flashed with fear as she heard their mother groaning her way up the stairs, asking why, for the hundredth time, she had had children. "Quick," Rachel said pushing Ginsberg by the hips, "back in the room before my mother sees you."

Ginsberg stood his ground, "You mean our mother?"

"My mother, your mother, our mother, what does it matter? She can't see you. Get in there." He slipped behind the door and Rachel inserted herself between him and their mother who had made it to the top of the stairs but had taken a moment to catch her breath. Ginsberg looked down at Rachel. From this angle, the morning sun streaming from the hall window made her blouse irrelevant. He could see every curve of his sister's body and he instinctively looked at his feet. When he glanced up, his eyes met Rachel's; she looked down, too.

By this time, their mother had caught her breath. "Rachel, why didn't you answer me? Is he up? Does he know Mr. Taxin is coming here to 'fire his ass'? Such language that Mr. Taxin has. Please tell me he is sick. Please tell me there is something wrong, God forbid. What are we going to do? We need the money with your father's health. Rachel, why are you standing there? What's inside? Is he? Is he? Oh, my God. My God! My God!" his mother covered her mouth and cried. Rachel moved out in the hall to comfort her. Ginsberg tried not to watch her walk away.

"Mama. He is fine. Everything is fine. Everything is wonderful. Calm down. Calm down. You'll see."

Ginsberg stepped out into the hallway. "Mama," he said in the Swede's voice. "Mama, it's me. A wonderful thing happened last night." His mother cocked her head to the left as if he were speaking Swedish as well. This man who looked nothing like her son. But Rachel moved behind Ginsberg and wrapped her arms around his waist affectionately. Rachel was peaking out from behind Ginsberg and nodding. Her eyes were shining as if she'd found a kitten and was asking if she could keep it.

Despite the fact Ginsberg in no way resembled himself and in no way sounded like himself, there wasn't as much turmoil in the house as you might imagine. Pleasant surprise described his mother's reaction. She stared at him with her mouth slightly open; she felt like a child pressing her face against the window of a toy store and being told by a typically strict parent that yes, she could go and get a doll.

She said nothing at first. Why would this man pretend to be him? There was certainly nothing to be gained by pretending to be her son. They had so little money. If this man standing in front of her in her son's ill-fitting pajamas wanted money, he would have to get in line behind them. And, let's face it, her son's earning power was his best feature. Finding no argument to the contrary, she could only conclude that he was her son and something had occurred last night.

But what had happened? Nothing short of a miracle. After a lifetime of tireless devotion to her family without so much as a thank you, why a miracle now? And why for him? What had he done to deserve it? He was all right, but nothing special. She shrugged and stopped thinking about it for fear of insulting God. This was just another thing in a long line of things she would have to accept. The only difference was that it was a good thing. She looked at this handsome man standing in front of her and, for some reason, didn't feel old any more. She ran her fingers through her hair trying to tame her dusty red curls.

Others might find it distasteful to be the object of one's mother and sister's desire but not Ginsberg. His inevitable rejection of them was only a small repayment for the grief they caused him all his life. He promised to let them down easy, but they had to understand that he was now clearly out of their league. He stroked his well-formed chin and smiled at them with patience and pity.

Downstairs the doorbell rang and his father, always a nervous man, shouted he would get it. Ginsberg heard the sound of his father's slippers scampering to the door so the person on the other side wouldn't have to wait any longer than he already had.

Ginsberg's father hated to disappoint people and he hoped he could regain his confidence by being servile. He claimed he was once a top salesman. But one day he showed up at the office of his oldest and best customer and saw the Cadillac of a competitor parked by his customer's; the cars looked like they were snuggling.

He felt betrayed. The anger burn inside of him and he was about to give them both hell, but found his legs wouldn't obey. He sat in his car and felt all his confidence drain out him like hot coffee in a styrofoam cup with a hole in it. What had he done to deserve his customer's infidelity? He looked at his eyes in the rear view mirror. Muddy green eyes, surrounded by wrinkles, looked at him with fear and pity. Who was he kidding? No one respected him. The only reason he got anywhere was his inability to take no for an answer. He wore people down like a millstone. He waited until his hands stopped shaking and pulled out of the parking lot and drove into obscurity. He was fired shortly thereafter and collected social security benefits due to a nervous condition.

Ginsberg became the sole support of his family by following his father into sales. His father would always come down to breakfast with dark rings under his eyes. He had not slept well, he would explain. He had been worrying whether his nervous attacks were genetic and Ginsberg would one day also lose his confidence and his job.

Ginsberg senior gasped when he threw open the door to see Ginsberg's boss accompanied by three men whom, Ginsburg senior was told, were representatives of the South America account. Mr. Taxin explained they were there to find out what catastrophe could have possibly happened to his "fuck up" of a son on this the most important, and possibly last, day of his career. Mr. Taxin pushed past the nearly catatonic Ginsberg senior and made his way into the living room.

Ginsberg senior swung like an unhinged pendulum between the four visitors seeking pity. Mr. Taxin was a short man with an enormous stomach. His head was bare except for the wiry brown hair that circled his freckled head, making him look like some sort of alien seed-pod about to burst. His tie knot disappeared into his dewlap-like throat. Large sweat stains were evident everywhere on his French blue striped shirt. There was nothing appealing about Mr. Taxin except his ability to intimidate.

Mr. Taxin pushed past Ginsberg senior and roamed about the first floor like a bloodhound on the trail of failure. The South American men wore enormous beards and would have looked at home on a box of cough drops. They spoke a foreign language that Ginsberg senior didn't understand. They nodded as they walked past him and sat down on the edge of the couch waiting to see what would happen next, and not-so-secretly enjoying the promised carnage.

"Well," Mr. Taxin asked as he waddled out from the kitchen, "where the fuck is the corpse? There had better be a corpse." Ginsberg senior was dizzy and tried to point upstairs, but only managed to indicate that Ginsberg was somewhere above sea level.

Mr. Taxin assaulted the staircase but stopped halfway when he came face-to-face with Ginsberg. Actually he came face-to-crotch with Ginsberg. Taxin quickly looked down at Ginsberg's large and well-formed feet.

As usual Taxin had planned to push by whomever or whatever was in his way. He wanted to strangle what life remained in Ginsberg. But he was prevented by a body that was like a wall, separating him from what he was and what he never would be.

Taxin's eyes slowly crawled up Ginsberg's body, from the feet, to the calves, past the thigh's, lingering too long on Ginsberg's midsection, which he regarded with a combination of admiration and jealousy, and up and over Ginsberg's chest. He considered Ginsberg's prominent and statuesque chin and then his lips, curled like those of an eagle spying a mouse running across the prairie. The nose did have an aquiline hook to it, making Taxin feel vulnerable and appetizing.

Taxin was confused and could not form a coherent thought. He bit his lips and decided to sweat more forcefully. "Ex. . .excuse me," was all that came out. He couldn't decide how to get out of the stranger's way. He was too fat for the man to go by without rubbing against him. He wouldn't dream of turning around and he was afraid of embarrassing himself more by tumbling down the stairs backwards. He stayed put out of inertia.

Ginsberg looked down at Taxin. It was inconceivable this man could have intimidated him. He was a nothing. Why hadn't he noticed this before? The chances were good he would lose his job. And, Ginsberg admitted with the ease of a spring morning, who cares? His job no matter how many nights it haunted his dreams was basically meaningless. He sold carbonation, the stuff inside bubbles; you couldn't get more trivial than that. The pay was lousy. The bonus opportunities were like the mechanical rabbit at a dog race. Ginsberg had always been close, but never quite earned the "generous bonuses" promised in the classified ad. He had always suspected Taxin, who now resembled a lump of damp clay, received a bonus for the number of bonuses he did not distribute.

"Looking for me?" Ginsberg said through his strong white teeth. Taxin tilted his head and wiped his forehead with the back of his hand. He opened his mouth, but nothing came out. Ginsberg started down the stairs and Taxin was forced to retreat backwards, like a dog shying from a fight.

As they reached the bottom of the stairs, Ginsberg looked over at the bearded guests who had discovered a bowl of fruit on the coffee table. One was eating a pear and the other was peeling a banana. The third was trying to open a pineapple with a thick thumbnail. "Ah, the gentlemen from South America," Ginsberg said as he pushed aside Taxin, who was wobbling next to shaky Ginsberg senior.

Ginsberg strode over to his guests who had instinctively stood at attention as if they were greeting the victor of a coup. Ginsberg took each hand and introduced himself. It was a pleasure to meet them and he was sure that this deal was merely the first of many to come.

The South American guests nodded their head at everything Ginsberg said, even if it was not a question. They did not speak English, but they understood power. They were eager to sign whatever Ginsberg put in front of them.

"Then we are agreed," Ginsberg held his hand out and they enthusiastically shook it and thanked him numerous time. "Fine. Let me get some clothes on and we will draw up the documents later at the office. Please take the fruit. You're quite welcome."

The gentlemen from South America smiled broadly and left thanking him with bowing movements on their way out. They never said anything to Taxin who was relying on Ginsberg senior to keep him from falling.

It did not take Taxin long to figure what happened. Not only had Ginsberg been transformed into the type of man that he could only dream of being, he had just achieved his bonus for the year. And with it, Taxin's own chance for a bonus flew away. This would not end well for him. He had sent too many people into obscurity not to recognize its stench.

On the road of life, Taxin turned into a cul-de-sac. Beyond the well-manicured lawns that encircled him, he could see happy, successful families sunning themselves by their pools. This was not a place for a person like him. He could only drive around the circle slowly and be on his way.

Ginsberg recognized the look on Taxin's face. He knew it well. It was the same look he had on his face for thirty-eight years worth of mornings before this one.

But now he had a new face—one built for success. While he knew the pain and frustration his boss must be experiencing, he could not find the smallest grain of pity for him. If forced to offer a conciliatory word, Ginsberg would shrug his wide shoulders and say that these things happen and the best thing to do is to accept it and move on. Absent a miracle, there is nothing to be done.

Standing in the living room, Taxin realized he was now as irrelevant as a bug. The best he could do was to leave silently and hope no one would see him go. He straightened his tie feigning residual dignity and went straight for the open door. He tripped over the welcome mat and fell on his face, spilling change on the driveway. He walked away without saying anything or picking up the coins.

...

After he had emerged, time contracted for Ginsberg into a state of perpetual summer. Half a year had passed and Ginsberg was already the largest distributor of carbonation on the East Coast, having swallowed all competitors including his former employers rapidly.

He kept Taxin around. Perhaps as some sort of a "memento mori," reminding him of who he had been. Now that he was a success, it was difficult to know what adversity and disappointment felt like. Try as he might, he could not fail, because no one wanted to see the rules of the game changed no matter how much they resented them. Standing by the plate glass window of his second floor office, Ginsberg watched all the people who used to populate his world. From this vantage point, they looked like ants. Every so often one would glance up and look at him. He knew they all hated him but also wished they could be him.

Perhaps he should tell them what it is like to live a life without envy and aspiration.

His cell phone buzzed, but he didn't answer it. It was his fiancée, Susan, telling him how her appointment went at the ob-gyn. Susan was a tall blonde who was also a corporate lawyer. She had stalked him at the gym and before he knew it, they were the golden couple, handsome, smart, and thoroughly in love. They would lie in their big bed in the middle of their downtown loft and she would stroke his cheeks and tell him how excited she was to be having his baby.

He tried to worry that the child would come out looking like his old self. But he could not sustain the obsession. Of course, it would be a pink and beautiful baby.

Although he had everything he wanted and more, he felt he forgotten something important. It buzzed around the back of his mind, like an ancient curse.

His parents kept his room the way it had been when he left. They told him it was a place for him to find some peace in his hectic life. He was touched and bemused. It had never been a

Shangri-La before, why shouldn't it be one now? But Ginsberg felt a need to visit every so often.

Once he saw a man who bore a striking resemblance to who he had been. The man also noticed Ginsberg and stopped to stare. They looked at each other from across the street, but did not make any effort to cross. What could they say to each other?

The man was smiling and muttering to himself. And then he started laughing. What could this gnome find so funny? Disturbed, Ginsberg walked away, lost in thought. He wanted to get to his parent's house as quickly as possible to confirm what he saw in his mirror that morning in the loft. His chin, which had been concrete hard, seemed somewhat softer, less defined. He touched it and it gave just a bit.

Maybe it was the light in the loft. Maybe it had been his imagination. But the man's laughter unnerved him and he ran to his parent's house.

He sprinted up the front stairs. He paused with his hand on the doorknob, listening to his family scurry like cockroaches anticipating his arrival.

Mulligan

God, I hate golf. I have never developed any proficiency at it beyond a healthy slice—a sickening arc to the right and out of sight. The ball, off on its own, free to hit who knows what or whom?

I'm never comfortable on a golf course; they are for Protestants or man's men. Or, in other words, not me. Me on the golf course is like an alien dropped from space with no way to communicate or go home.

I have crafted a catalogue of reasons for not playing golf, from a shoulder injury of undetermined seriousness and duration to a perpetually terminal uncle who needs to be watched so my aunt can get some rest. My boss is exasperated when I arrive late to company golf outings and leave early, all because of spontaneous flooding in my apartment.

But how do you say no when your best friend calls the morning of a charity event for the blind and asks you to be in his foursome? Mark says he's desperate. His boss is on the board of directors and he's in charge of finding two other players. Number four broke his foot the day before and has yet to develop the ability to play on crutches. I owe him for too many favors to enumerate. Besides, this is for a good cause—blind people, can't I see that?

I dig out the clubs my brother gave me years ago when he bought his überclubs. He regards me as a charity case—an Eliza Doolittle with a five iron or some sort of heretic waiting to be baptized in a water hazard. He has fantasies of the two of us playing together as we age—two old men, sharing secrets. But I already know about the weekend in Hilton Head with his co-worker.

The clubs are dusty and I find a sock in the bag that I thought I lost years ago; unfortunately I tossed its match. I tell my wife Shelly, who is still in bed where I'm going. She opens one eye, rolls it, predicting that this day cannot end well.

Mark's boss is one of those people who define life in terms of golf. I wouldn't be surprised if he calls heaven "the club house." Anything else is mere interruption. He extracts each club from the bag as if he were a doctor delivering a baby. He lists the famous courses he has played. He stares hard into my eyes through wire-frame glasses to detect recognition. I nod and blink a lot.

Mark laughs at every inside joke about doglegs on the seventh hole of the McWhatever course in Scotland. The other man is jovial enough. I didn't catch his name and am too embarrassed to ask him to repeat it. He shows off a new driver that he is using for the first time. Mark and his boss look like they want to masturbate over it. I say cool and purse my lips like I mean it.

My shot off the first tee is respectable, sailing a fair distance in the general direction of the flag and landing on the fairway. Have I suddenly been blessed with the ability to swing a golf club? Or am I being set up for even greater disappointment? My second shot confirms my second supposition.

It is not so much a slice, but a repudiation of everything

straight. The ball's arc is a wobbly rainbow thirty feet forward and a hundred yards into the woods. The three of us watch it tumble into the pine tree branches as if it is a UFO streaking from the sky. Three pairs of eyes turn towards me in the assumption I have injured myself. There can be no other explanation.

But there was. I hate golf and golf hates me. Swinging my three iron over my shoulder, I venture off into the woods.

Somewhere behind me there is laughter. Mark's boss says something like, "It looks like you have to use a mulligan already." And then more laughter.

If I could get away with it, I would keep walking through the woods to whatever is on the other side. I would leave my clubs behind; it wouldn't matter, there's no chance I am going to use them again. But Mark needs me and I feel some responsibility to look for my lost ball. There's nothing that says I have to be quick about it.

The woods are at least ten degrees cooler than the fairway. I swing my club back and forth as if I am clearing underbrush. I find all sorts of things in the weeds—pop cans, empty fifths of cheap whiskey, condom wrappers, and parts of an engine. But no ball.

If only I had been smart enough to pocket a ball before I went for my walk in the woods. It doesn't matter if I cheat; there's no way I am going to finish anything better than fourth.

I know there's a time limit for looking for a ball and some procedure if the ball could not be found. But for the life of me, I cannot remember what they are. I'll continue to look for the ball until they come and find me.

"Look's like you are going to have to take a mulligan," a voice like sandpaper says behind me. Startled, I spin around nearly smacking her in the face with my club.

She's about five foot three with a pear-shaped body topped by a small head dominated by large, plastic red-framed glasses that she wears around her neck with a woven cord. She has a turkey-like neck around which she wears a necklace made of large

Bakelite beads. She is dressed in black velour.

She's also somewhat transparent as I can see the bushes swaying behind her. She's not quite there. Instead of frightening me, I feel a strange kinship with her. Most of the time I don't feel like I'm quite here either. It's like I am controlled by someone with a remote control who is nearly out of range.

She's chewing gum and staring into space. I'm not sure she's talking to me.

"Where did you come from?"

She jams her thumb over her left shoulder. "Over there." Over there was a thicket of brambles, tightly packed trees and some sort of marsh.

"Over there?"

She nods.

"Why are you here?"

She gave a diaphanous shrug and said nothing.

I try again. "Why are you're here?" I have more luck this time.

"I am looking for you."

"Me? Do I know you?"

"No," she says, pauses, then adds, "It's your turn."

"What does that mean, my turn?"

"It means you're next."

"Next for what?"

"Next to be served." This conversation, if you could call it that, is going nowhere.

"I'm Adam," I say, holding out my hand. I realize too late to escape embarrassment that there was no way for us to shake hands. It would have been like shaking hands with a cloud. "And you are?"

"We are not authorized to give out our names. It doesn't matter any way. I am here to help." She seemed to have a different definition for "help."

"Help me? Why?"

She turns and floats back towards the brambles.

"Wait, where are you going?"

"Back there," she says.

"I'm sorry if I insulted you."

"You didn't insult me. I thought you didn't want my help."

"I do. I mean I guess I do. What are you offering?"

"A second chance."

"A second chance? Who are you? Are you an angel?"

She shrugs as if she doesn't understand the question and tries again. "It's your turn. Everybody supposed to get a turn. But we can't get to everybody before they die. Cutbacks." She rolls her eyes in experienced despair. "These days we are lucky if we can clear thirty percent."

"What does my turn entail? Riches? Fame?"

She sighs like the breeze. "You get a second chance." She looks at my golf club. "It's like a life mulligan."

"A mulligan?" I ask. I pull out the small piece of paper that cost me five bucks at check in. Standing here in the middle of weeds after the first hole, I probably should have taken the five for twenty dollars. "Is this what you are talking about?"

She nods and stares at me expectantly.

"That's it? That's all I get? A chance to reshoot?"

"If that's what you choose."

"What do you mean, 'if that's what I choose?' What other choice is there?"

She looks like she was late for a coffee break. "If you want to use it for a golf game, that's fine. You wouldn't be the first to do it."

"What other people choose?"

"Some people choose a different job. Some people choose to marry someone else. Some people even decide to go all the way back to childhood and start over."

"You mean I can change one thing in my life?"

"If it's been done, it can be undone." She tries to smile warmly, but looks like she has indigestion.

So what to choose? My first inclination is to get the hell out of the golf game. I could go back to this morning and not answer the phone. But that would be a waste of this opportunity.

The next thing that comes to mind is never working for Murphy Materials. The irony that I work for a company that sells fake pavers is not lost on me. All day long I promote the natural look of our faux stone. But I have no enthusiasm to excel so I can find something better. Most of the time I just try to fade into the background so my boss doesn't see me. It's a vicious circle—loaf, resent, lather, repeat.

What if I could snap my finger and be free? I could have stayed at Republic Windows. Sure, I was bored, but not overtaxed. In hindsight, it wasn't so bad, was it?

But what was so good about selling windows? The pay was bad, the work dull and the status nonexistent. What makes me so sure the grass would be greener there? It wasn't before. Clearly this opportunity needs a bit more consideration. "I am sorry this is taking so long. Is there a time limit?"

She's been gnawing on one of her cuticles and says, "No, take as long as you would like. I'm paid by the hour." It is becoming clearer why they are so far behind on fulfillment.

There's shouting behind me. The remaining members of my foursome are becoming impatient. Mark stands at the edges of the woods urging me to take the damn mulligan already. "Is there any way we can continue this conversation later," I ask her, "I'm in the middle of a game."

She puts down her thumb and shrugs. "Sure," she says, "but I will have to go on to the next person on the list. It's policy. I will get back to you at my earliest convenience." And by earliest convenience, she clearly meant never.

"I'll be right back," I say. "Don't go anywhere."

She shrugs and pulls out a thermos from beneath her vest. She sits on a fallen tree, sipping something out of the cap.

I run to the edge of the woods and find Mark who is nervously waving at his boss and friend. "Where the hell have you been," he asks. "Since when do you give a fuck about a golf ball?"

"Look, I can't explain right now, but is there any way you can get me out of the rest of the game?"

"What are you talking about? My boss is nuts when it comes to golf. There is nothing and I mean nothing more sacred to him than golf. And now you want me to tell you are pulling out on the first hole? Jesus, I'll be fired by the back nine."

"Look, I'm really sorry. Something has come up. Something really important. I wouldn't ask unless it was important. I did you a favor by agreeing to play in the first place."

"Some favor, you played all of 90 yards."

"I know. You are just going to have to trust me. I can't let this chance go by."

He looks over my shoulder, but can't see anything through the trees. "What you got in there?" He narrows his eyes and adds, "or who?" This is funny coming from him as he goes through women like Kleenex. He says none are the "one" for him. He speaks of "the one" in reverential tones as if they kept missing each other. But I think he only created her as a way to get sympathy and, as a result, more women.

What can I say? That I am talking with some sort of bureaucratic spirit who has offered me the chance to change my life?

Who knows if, when all is said and done, he would make the cut? Mark has been my closest friend since kindergarten. He is best when he is at his worst; participating in a round of bile-swallowing jealousy of all those we feel are completely undeserving of whatever good luck they stumble across. But what would happen if my life changed? Who will be my bitch partner? But, then again, if I make the necessary corrections, what would there be to bitch about? Sorry, Mark.

He looks back over his shoulder at our group and then asks quietly, "It's a woman, right?"

I look him in the eye and say, "Yes." There's no need to lie.

"What are you going to tell Shelly?"

"Hopefully nothing."

"You sure you want to do this? Think about the consequences."

"You should talk. Remember the Sheehan Twins? How long did you think you could get away with it?"

"I told you they weren't the one. Besides I'm not the one who is married. You sure you want to do this?"

"Yes."

"Okay, limp back into the woods. I'll tell them you hurt your leg and are going to the hospital. They'll be impressed I decided to continue playing golf rather than help my friend. Good luck, man. I hope you know what you are doing." He turns and walks slowly back toward the first hole. He stops halfway and, seeing me looking at him, raises a fist in solidarity.

I watch him walk off. He's a true friend. I'm going to miss him.

She is still sitting on the log when I got back. She is fading into the background and I almost walk right through her. She doesn't flinch and stares at me with half-closed eyes.

With slow and deliberate movements, she asks, "Are you ready?"

I am not. I had planned to go back to my freshman year of college, smoke a lot less pot and not waste my time believing my success as Tevye in the high school production of "Fiddler" was a sign of great theatrical things to come.

This time I would spend more of my time on the science side of the campus. Less time trying to get people to buy me beer and more time in the library.

But there's the problem of junior year chemistry in high school. No matter how much more I would have studied in college, it was built on an unsteady foundation from my teen years. No medical school would accept me when I barely passed rudimentary chemistry. They wouldn't be swayed by the excuse that something wonderful happened to girls' bodies between tenth and eleventh grade. There's no reprieve for horniness. No, clearly I will need to go further back. And further back probably means no Shelly, my wife of eleven years.

My throat constricts as it did when I said goodbye to my college girlfriend, Andrea, after graduation. When "I'll call you soon" meant, "Have a good life."

Andrea was a true wild child with shoulder-length dirty blonde hair and a preference for my flannel shirts and baggy jeans. Andrea and I had known each other since freshman year and I had been merely a friend until a trip to see the Grateful Dead in Nashua. A few beers, a tab of acid, and one too few sleeping bags later we were a couple.

Andrea described the transformation: "I never had your tongue in my mouth." Unfortunately for me, Andrea had seen a side of me that had been born and died that night and was as unfamiliar to me as it had been to her.

It was exhausting being him. He was the type who considered riding roller coasters while drunk as barely passable for fun. Some days I would lie next to her in bed staring at the ceiling, feeling my heart pound wildly as chemically-altered blood weakened my arteries.

We broke up at least ten times when I showed no interest in going to parties, poetry readings. or hitchhiking to Boston. She would stare at me as if something had invaded my body and replaced me with moss. But a few beers later or a couple tokes and make-up sex would make up for my dullness.

I dropped Andrea off in Pittsburgh for graduate school and ignored her letters and phone calls and never picked up the box from the post office that I was sure contained the books and tapes I had given her. I was too exhausted to feel guilty.

That was why I love Shelly so much. She loves me for who I am. What she saw when we first met was what she got—a bookish, neurotic, balding male with an overabundance of average body parts.

She is without a doubt the most forgiving person I have ever met. She is committed to empathy the way a nun is committed to Christ. People are naturally drawn to her because the more damaged they are, the more she likes them.

I have never felt so truly myself as I do when I am with Shelly. When she tells me she loves me, I feel loveable. Holding my hand in hers is the closest I feel to being in utero. All my doubts and anxiety melt when my fingers are entwined with hers.

But cashing in my mulligan means changing me. Changing me is changing the man she loved. In theory she could grow to love this new man, but I don't want her to. If I would be truly happy with myself, there would be no need for her sympathy.

There would be too much pressure to be someone I wasn't. She would treat me like some sort of patient who had a stroke or Alzheimer's. She would constantly try to love me back to who I was. It would be better to walk away. I am sure she would find another emotional vagabond to adopt and love.

I look over at the spirit, who is bored—Department of Motor Vehicles bored. There's no need to move the line along. It would be there tomorrow and the next day.

A bird flies by and it grabs her attention as it flies to the ground, picks up a twig, and returns to the branch on which it is industriously building a nest. She watches it not out of fascination or appreciation, but because she needs somewhere to rest her eyes. It could be a forest fire, a laughing baby, or paint drying.

I go further back to middle school. A rush of embarrassing memories floods my mind: long, greasy hair, thick plastic-frame glasses, and a tendency to pick my nose whenever the most popular girl in school happened to be coming around the corner. Combined with an interest in socialist politics in a very conservative suburb, I was soon inducted in the hermit society.

So where did I veer off the road? When did I ever like being me?

There was a time. Around first grade. It was autumn but the

wind was still warm, the only sounds the wind rustling the leaves and a cocker spaniel snuffling through the grass. A girl with dark brunette hair and pig tails stares at me with dark eyes. Her nose is perky and her cheeks are freckled.

We stare at each other after she tells me she is moving to a place called Texas. Texas is as mysterious as the feelings of loneliness and desperation that accompany the news. In the future this feeling will mutate into rejection and frustration. But for now, it is like putting on a favorite coat for the first time. It feels odd yet familiar.

She tells me her father got a new job and she's moving before Christmas. What do I feel? Confusion mixed with a vague sense of the inevitable. It's the birth of disappointment that will be my constant companion, conjured by the freckled face of a first grader in pigtails.

If we had been older, there might have a futile attempt to fumble in someone's bedroom. Or if we were even older, as old as I am now, there would be a hug held for a second or two longer than usual. We would exchange promises to keep in touch, knowing full well that we will be lucky to exchange a couple of e-mails and trust in Facebook to maintain our friendship.

But this was a farewell without the vocabulary to express the enormous loss we were unaware we would experience.

If Evie had stayed, how long would it be before I would be pulling her hair and calling her names, all in the hope that she would notice me? All through elementary school, people would think it was cute we wanted to have play dates and were the only member of the opposite sex invited to our birthday parties.

In middle school, we'd be brother and sister, except without the arguments. Would it be sixth grade that we would finally hold each other's hands walking across an empty golf course in winter? Our fingers would embrace without comment, like a handshake after agreeing to a friendship that was more than just friends.

It would be months before our first kiss. Grabbed in

midsentence with absolutely no grace or skill. Just simply pressing two sets of chapped lips together, quickly. And then something that sounds like "I love you."

High school would bring a public acknowledgement of our relationship. And from there college across the state from each other with weekend visits and then marriage and happily ever after.

Evie leaving my life was the birth of regret. Regret that became the kernel on which disappointment and doubt lumped together like a comet. If Evie didn't leave, there would be nothing to attach to.

There's the crisp sound of something breaking through the trees behind me. I turn just in time to see a golf ball flying towards my head. I duck and it lands halfway between the spirit and me. She doesn't seem to notice.

Sounding like elephant in the brush, a fat man, dressed in a Budweiser sweater vest and white shorts walking towards us, swinging his club. He's muttering to himself as he roots around the weeds.

The spirit looks unconcerned. But I panic. There's not time to think about it any longer. Turning to my spirit I say, "Take me back to when Evie Wheaton left Illinois. Please don't let her leave."

I am six, and standing on a street next to a pig-tailed, freckle-faced girl. "My Dad told me we almost moved to Texas. But we're not going," she says.

"I'm glad."

Evie looks down the street. We watch a six-year-old Mark in a big, puffy coat, waddling toward us.

"I'm going camping with my dad and brother," Mark says to me. Mark never looks at Evie. He gets real nervous around her. He walks down the street, and her eyes follow him.

"I think Mark's cute," Evie says. "I'm going to marry him someday.

The Bruegel Birthday Kompany

Naomi has a subscription to most every parenting magazine still in print. On every page smiling parents beam at appreciative children. Everyone has golden hair, good teeth, perfect skin, and clear consciences. Naomi reads every word, then leaves articles on my nightstand to help me grasp the importance of patience, spending quality time with my offspring, and the deleterious affects of foul language on young minds. If only I followed their advice I would not only be a better father, I would enjoy being one more.

    For my part, I think bears have the right idea. Sorry son, it's been nice knowing you, but there's a tree with your name on it. See ya.

    Lucas and I got off on the wrong foot. From the day he was born, I was already behind. He hated being held by me and I hated holding him. From the word go, parenthood was like ill-fitting clothes.

I was surprised how inept I was at being a father. I always thought I would be the fun parent, but each time I walked into the room and saw Naomi and Lucas giggling, fun was sucked out of the room. Shaving in the bathroom, cringing as Lucas screamed from his crib, I looked at myself in the mirror and had no idea who was looking back at me.

They say the time flies when you have children. But if you don't have any fun, it staggers like the way Lucas drags his feet whenever we are running late. Seven years have passed to Naomi's surprise and my chagrin. She looks backwards; I am counting down the eleven more years until I can throw him out. And now it was time for his birthday and my annual argument with Naomi over what is appropriate for a child's birthday party.

In the past few years, birthdays have gone from a gathering of adult friends, complete with juice boxes and beer, cupcakes and ribs to an undeclared competition to produce the most elaborate celebration of one revolution of the Earth circling around the sun. Clowns are hired. Balloon animals are made. All parties are given with the generous spirit of a gladiator fight. If a folk singer entertained at Janie's birthday, a power trio would be on the bill for Jeremy's.

Naomi comes home from each party, lugging the goody booty, biting her lip knowing the gauntlet had been thrown down. With Lucas's party rapidly approaching, we had better figure something spectacular so as not to embarrass him or incur exorbitant therapist expenses in the future.

"It's his seventh birthday," she hisses as we sit at the kitchen table, sifting through the numerous birthday planning web sites on our laptops. "It's an important birthday," she says in her don't-even-think-about-contradicting-me voice. "So far there have been Zoe's pony rides, Claire's laser tag, and Tenzing's pool party. How is Lucas going to feel if we don't do something nice for him?"

I shrug, remembering my seventh birthday. I think it involved red plastic fire helmets, cupcakes, and playing spin the bottle when my parents were out of the room. I remember really wanting to kiss the girl with long, brown hair and freckles on her nose. I ended up kissing Jenny, a pudgy blonde who had been kissed by every boy sometime during that year.

I don't want you to think Naomi is crazy. She is merely crazy about Lucas. She had a distant father and a mother who was obsessed with her career as a realtor. She remembers feeling like an inconvenience throughout her childhood. When we had Lucas after two years of trying, she swore he would never feel unwanted. I, too, was an only child and was, according to Naomi, spoiled by anxious parents. Maybe that is why Lucas and I don't get along. Neither of us likes to share.

When she's in these moods, I stay out of her way. It is easier to let her spoil Lucas, which gets me out of a lot of parenting duties. I call it a win-win.

But some of the suggestions she has for his party are obscene. What parent is going to let their kid go up in a hot air balloon? And what seven-year-old kid is interested in a fondue party? All I could see was spilled cheese and melted fingers.

Naomi sighs her special sigh, which means I am not helping and tells me to come up with some suggestions of my own. Plastic hats and empty wine bottles are out of the question. For the time being, she is the only girl Lucas is allowed to kiss.

I pick up a copy of Chicago Parent magazine from the summer. Naomi had dog-eared the issue with possible suggestions for the "perfect party for your child." I skip every one of them as if they are talking to someone else. Toward the back of the magazine, after a lame column on parenting humor, I find a little ad, surrounded by a thick black line. Printed in a vaguely Gothic font was:

The Bruegel Birthday Kompany. Children's Parties. Occult Supplies. 1118 W. Fulton Mkt. Open Monday thru Wed. 8:45 am – 1:00 pm, Thursday 6:00 pm – 7:15 pm. Or by appointment.

There's no telephone number or email address, only a small line drawing of a shrunken head with its eyes, nostrils and mouth sewn shut.

"What about this place?" I ask, holding the magazine up.

Naomi rolls her eyes and makes a face.

"I'm serious. It looks cool."

"It looks repulsive," she says.

"He'll be the talk of the class."

"Every parent will hate us. That thing," she says, shoving her chin toward the shrunken head, "gives me the willies. God knows what else they have in that place. Probably full of rats and fleas."

"Still, it would be cool."

"I don't find infecting children cool. Move on."

Naomi goes back to searching web sites and gives me the choice of a pottery party or a space camp theme. I tell her it doesn't matter to me. She mutters, "It never matters to you."

I let it go. I look at my watch. It's Thursday and nearly 5:00 pm. The Bruegel Birthday Kompany opens in little more than an hour. Since Lucas is at soccer practice and would be busy with piano lessons after that, there's no need to worry I would be missed.

Fulton Market is one of those locations where you can watch history march by. It used to be full of meat-rendering plants. On every corner are fading pictures of smiling cows and pigs that probably didn't fool the animals on their way to slaughter.

Several of the buildings had been converted to housing and have optimistic names like Coventry Lane and Millennium Place, each promising new heights in urban living. Their faded signs indicate bad timing. The area looks like the welcoming center for the apocalypse.

1118 West Fulton Market is announced simply by three metal "ones" and the echo of the number eight, now gone, incised in the many layers of paint. Small gold letters stuck to the door spell out "Th Brue e   irth ay K mpany". I look down and see a small "d" lying in the leaves. I pick up and try to stick it back on. It lingers for a moment and then flutters down.

I try the doorknob; it doesn't budge. I look at my watch. It's 6:10. I lean against the door, but it refuses to move. There's a small doorbell button that looks broken. The button is stuck half way in, leaning towards the right. I push it, but doubt it's connected to anything. Underneath the doorbell someone had written in ballpoint pen. I brush the cobwebs aside and read "KNOCK LOUD."

It is almost 6:15 before I hear anything stirring on the other side of the door. It's an indecipherable noise at first; just a thump, thump. But then it morphs into thump, thump, "Coming." And finally thump, thump, "I'm coming," scrape. Thump, thump, scrape. The door shudders and I step back. The disagreeable lock shivers and eventually concedes; the door opens slightly.

Half of a face—one eye behind thick aviator glasses, a nostril, the left side of mouth and beard—appears about a foot below my head. "Sorry, we're closed," he says in a friendly tone. His voice sounds like a 72-rpm record. He would have shut the door if I did not shove my left arm into the breech, showing him my watch.

"No, you aren't. You're supposed to be open."

"I am? Well thank you for telling me. Sometimes I forget." He opens the door and the odor that rolls out is a combination of sweat, bowel, cardamom, and mothballs. I hear the same thumping and scraping noise as he closed the door again and unhitches the security chain.

The door opens as if by magic, but I discover him on the other side holding onto the doorknob. I am looking straight down at his scalp. He has grey hair that is kept a tad long for his age (around sixty). He wears a bushy beard that covers his throat. The first obvious thing about him is that if he were standing straight up (which he isn't) he would be barely five feet tall. The second is the ancient, heavy apparatus of metal braces over his brown corduroy pants. He holds twin wooden canes, one in his left hand and one hanging from his left wrist. He holds the doorknob for stability.

He has a smile that is simultaneously welcoming and predatory. He looks down at his canes. "Polio," he says.

"Polio?"

"I had religious parents," he said, making the cuckoo sign by his temple with his right hand. "It's a pain in the ass. Come in. Come in," he beckons me in. He transfers one cane to his right hand.

He has a peculiar method of walking. He plants his left cane about a foot in front of him and then his right cane. He drags his legs forward. The tops of his leather boots are scuffed. It takes him nearly five minutes to make it the twenty feet to the counter, which gives me ample time to look around.

The store had once been a Chinese laundry and/or a parts store. There is a colored calendar from 1974 with a picture of a woman in a traditional Chinese costume. Just to the left of the beaded curtain that leads to the back room is a schematic drawing of an antique washing machine, complete with an exploded view of the wringer assembly.

There is a collection of boxes on the shelves that line the back wall. Each box has a label, but the writing is faded and illegible. There is also a ticket dispenser as if it is needed. He sees me looking at the dispenser and says, "Don't worry, it's empty."

He moves the stool with one of his canes, and bracing himself against the counter, he begins to ascend with the precision of an alpinist. It is quite an endeavor and I say nothing for fear of disturbing his concentration. I didn't want to have to pick him off the floor.

When he reaches the summit, he is panting and sweating. He tries to speak several times, but can't. When he finally talks, after mopping his face numerous times with a yellowed handkerchief, his voice is strained and quiet. And yet despite all the effort, he has a pleasant smile. "Now, how can I help you? Exorcism? Curse? Talisman?"

I shake my head. "Children's party. For my son. He's seven."

He looks at me as if I was speaking Greek. "Children's party?"

"Yes. I saw your ad in Chicago Parent."

"I thought they stopped running that ad years ago. I told them to cancel it. They offered me a reduced rate and I offered them nothing. I guess they took my offer." He snorts.

"Does…does this mean you don't do children's party any more?"

"No, I still do them. What do you have in mind?"

"I don't know. Do you have a brochure or something I could look at?"

He bites his lip and rolls his eyes. "Oh Lord, if I do, I don't know where it is. I could tell you what I do and you tell me if you think your son would like one of them. Does that sound okay?"

I nod and shrug, and wonder if it's 7:15 yet.

"Let's see, does your son like bears?"

"What do you mean does he like bears? What kind of bears? You mean like teddy bears?"

He has a hard time not laughing. "No, I mean a real bear. Usually a brown bear or a black bear. I have to see what I have in stock."

"Is this some sort of petting zoo? For kids to pet?"

He laughs loudly, launching what looks like part of his dinner onto the counter. He doesn't seem to notice or mind. "Only if they want an arm ripped off."

"You don't mean a wild bear?"

"Of course I do. What would be the fun if it were tame? The dogs would simply kill it. Where would be the sport? Where would be the entertainment?"

We look at each other for a second or two. I try to detect irony in his face. He is waiting for me to give him a date. I give in first.

"You're kidding."

"No, I'm serious. If you have a tame bear people would howl. We use only wild bears." And then to answer a question he thinks I am about to ask. "But don't worry, we chain it to the ground with double strength chains. There's no chance of the bear breaking free. Of course, we ask you to give it wide berth, but I can assure you that your children will be completely safe so long as they stand outside the yellow line. Why are you laughing?"

"You've got be joking. Bear baiting? Is it legal? Is it ethical?"

He strokes his beard with the back of his left hand. "I suppose that is up to the individual. All I can say is that for vast periods of history and in some places in rural Pakistan today, the answer is a resounding yes. But legal or no, I can assure you, it will be a party not to be missed. And that's what you are after, aren't you?"

"I don't think the slaughter of an innocent bear is any thing to be proud of."

"Who said anything about the bear being innocent? It's a bear, for heaven's sake! If it weren't for the leather collar and the chains, it wouldn't think twice about ripping off your face. Innocent!"

"I think we will pass on bear baiting. We live in a condo, anyway. I'm pretty sure it is against condo laws. What else do you have?"

"I suppose cock fights are against the condo laws, too." He crosses his arms and exhales loudly through his nose as if he doesn't know what this country has come to.

"I am not going to have seven-year-old kids betting on cock fights."

"We don't use real money, we use candy. The kids love it. Beats a piñata any day."

"And you think kids would like to see an animal being killed?"

He leans forward and beckons me to come closer. I don't want to because I'm sure he smells of incontinence. But I lean in. Even on the high stool, he only comes up to my neck. "I know kids would love to see it."

"I would think they would run screaming and have nightmares for days on end."

He is unimpressed. "Some do. Sometimes most do. But you know what?" Now he bends over until I can feel his moustache rubbing against my ear. He whispers as if he is revealing some secret. "They all love it. It's better than any video games. Because the blood is real. And real beats fake any day. Every kid knows that. I know children who go to bed screaming every night because they can't get the thought of a dog eating a bear's entrails out of their head and then wake up in the morning asking to see it again."

"You would think the parents would complain or, worse, call the cops."

"You would think that, wouldn't you? But there are three types of parents. The first type never makes it through the door. They look at the door, at the neighborhood and at themselves. And they're gone. Out of sight, out of mind, as they say. The second type makes it through the door. Thinks I am joking. Is appalled that I am not. Can't believe what I am offering. Threatens to call the cops and leaves. But the cops never come. Why? I don't know. Maybe they think someone else will do it. Maybe they don't want to get involved. They may even be a bit ashamed that they ran away."

"And the third type?"

He looks at me a bit too long for my comfort. "The third says 'yes.' Not at first. Maybe with a little reluctance. Maybe they want it to all be a joke. But, in the end, they want it to be true. They want to see what's on the other side of the mirror."

"What mirror? What are you talking about?"

"Your kids. They are tiny mirrors on tiny legs. You don't want to admit it. Parents don't want to admit what kind of brutes they share their house with. They can be generous and kind, but deep down they wouldn't mind seeing somebody suffering. Just like their parents.

"You don't have kids, do you?"

"I never had the aptitude for children," he says, scratching the underside of his chin and then adds, "or the appetite. And before you ask, yes, I have had sex and with big women, too. They like it when I climb up their bodies. I spend more time on the ascent than a big man would." His smile makes me uncomfortable as if he is a cannibal deciding on a recipe.

He looks at his watch and notices that he will be closing in 20 minutes or so. "So cock fights are out as well?"

"Do the birds just fight or do they kill each other, too?" I knew the answer, but I didn't want him to think I was a wuss.

"Oh, they don't kill each other. It is really more like 'cock sparring.'" He presses his thumbs and index fingers together, like he is playing itsy bitsy spider. "We put little helmets on their heads and little boxing gloves on their little feet. And beak guards. Don't forget the beak guards. And then they circle and jab, jab and jab for five rounds. We use robins for corner men. And then the gloves come off and they shake wings and retire to the dressing room for a rub down. "It's quite a stirring display of sportsmanship. The kids go nuts for it." He nonchalantly crosses his arms and looks at me.

"Okay, I was being stupid. I just really don't think my son would like something dying. What do you have in the non-dying category?"

"Gladiator fights?"

"Gladiator fights as in two guys trying to stab each other?"

"Or brain each other with a cudgel, depends on their weapon of choice."

"I said no killing."

"But killing is completely optional. Think of it. Your son, little Jimmy, or whatever his name is, has complete control whether the loser is killed. Little thumbs up and he lives. Little thumbs down and he dies. Of course, there is an up charge if the thumb comes down. Gladiators aren't easy to find. But that is between you and me. Little Jimmy will never know and he will be the talk of school for weeks for having the coolest party ever," he pauses, raising his left eyebrow, "and the coolest dad. No killing necessary for a good time to be had by all."

He winks at me and adds as if he can't restrain himself, "You want to know something? They always want the loser killed. I've done this a bunch of times, but even the most squeamish kids eventually gives a thumbs down. People tell me it's peer pressure. There's always some kid who is going to egg the birthday boy on. But I don't think that's it. I think deep down, they want to see it. Wouldn't you, if given the choice?"

"No," I say, more to convince myself than anything. "Look, say what you want, I don't want anybody dying at my kid's party. So what else you got?"

He is confused. He jumps off his stool and lands with a thump. He disappears behind the counter. I lean over to see if he's okay, but I can't see him. His left hand appears above the countertop like a periscope. A periscope, I note, that had recently worn a wedding ring, but no longer. I can still see the furrow where it had been. I smile like a smug therapist.

I hear him rooting around beneath the counter; it's a cacophony of clinks, tearing paper, plastic lids being opened and closed, and something that sounds like an insect's whine. Every so often, the top of his head surfaces like some sort of aquatic creature belched up from the deep.

"Can I help in some way?" I ask his scalp, which shakes side to side.

"I am sure I can find something appropriate if you give me time. Believe it or not, it's been awhile since I did a kids party where something didn't die."

"Really? Am I really that different?

"Well, yes. Most are like you in the beginning. They blanch and belch and pretend to be horrified. But in the end, they give in. It's not me who's obscene; it's their hypocrisy. The more they complain in the beginning, the more they lean in close at the end as if they are trying to smell its final breath. Ah, I knew I would find it."

I hear him opening a heavy trunk with rusty hinges. There is rustling and then a small orange pompom appears, followed by a conical hat made of yellow felt with purple dots. He is wearing a clown's hat and a small rubber red ball for a nose. Neither had been worn lately as the hat has dust on it and the nose has dry rot.

"Well?" is all he says.

"What are you supposed to be?"

He pulls on his nose that is attached to elastic strings and looks at it. "I'm a clown, isn't it obvious?" When it isn't, he snaps the nose back and dust fills the air. He coughs and tries to explain. "Don't (cough) worry (cough) I have big (cough) shoes and baggy pants (cough), too. Once you see the (cough) the (cough) (cough) whole thing, it'll (cough) (cough) be better."

He holds up a stubby finger, turns his head and seems about to retch up an internal organ. His little shoulders quake with each cough and I wonder which one will be his last. I imagine him snapping to attention and then fall, board stiff, onto the floor, still wearing his hat and rubber nose. I start to laugh. I try to stifle it and end up only coughing, too.

He looks at me. His face is covered with all kinds of red splotches. His little conical hat is now jauntily listing towards the left and he has pushed his glasses onto his forehead. I laugh and cough harder. "Got to you, too?" he asks.

I nod, trying to erase the image of the police drawing a chalk outline of his body on the floor, including the triangle for the hat and a little circle for the red nose.

He clears his throat and spits the most revolting lugie next to him. How long would it be before he cleaned it up?

"So, I obviously need a new rubber nose. Don't worry, that's not extra. Just a cost of doing business."

"So you are going to come as a clown to my kid's birthday party? Isn't that a little predictable? What are you going to do, make animals out of balloons and tell silly jokes?" I am actually disappointed he hadn't offered anything more repulsive.

He shakes his head. "The only thing I can make out of balloons is a bunch of burst balloons. The jokes I know aren't suitable for kids and will probably prompt a lot of questions."

"So no balloons, no silly jokes? How about juggling or games that involve ping pong balls."

"Can't juggle. Don't have any ping pong balls."

"So what do you exactly do?"

"Well, I dress up like a clown and show up."

"And?"

"And let the kids have their way with me."

"What do you mean, have their way with you? You mean like beat you up?"

He nods slowly. "It usually takes less than fifteen minutes to go from 'oh, look, a clown' to 'let's steal his canes and see if he falls down.'"

"That's awful."

"It's a living."

"Don't the parents try to stop them?"

He shook his head. "No, They can't believe their little angel or prince is capable of snapping the suspenders of a dwarf with polio dressed as a clown. Some of them have this silly grin on their face, hoping no one is watching or, if they are, they hope no one is as mortified as they are. The other half can't believe how bad their kids are making them look. There's real fury in their eyes. If they could get away with it, they would choke the life out of Prince Angel."

"At the end of the party, I'm wearing most of the birthday cake. They're only too glad to pay me if I just go away and say nothing more about the whole thing. It's sad, really," he says as if he is announcing it's raining.

"So what are you trying to prove?"

"Prove? I am not trying to prove anything. I'm trying to make a living."

"By staging bear baiting, cock fights, gladiator battles and a game of torture the dwarf clown? Must be some point to it."

"There must be some point?" He rolls his eyes. "Haven't found one yet. Look, all I know is that people can be pretty rotten when they think no one is looking. And they are willing to pay me to keep the secret. Before you condemn me, why would you begrudge a poor cripple dwarf a chance to make some cash?"

"So this is some sort of revenge?"

"Revenge for what? Revenge for my polio? Revenge for being a dwarf? Revenge for my obsession with big tits that are usually out of my reach in oh, so many ways? Who has time for revenge? Save it for Sunday, I always say." He narrows his eyes in much the same way a bird of prey locates a scurrying rodent on the prairie below. "So how can I help you?"

He pushes a sheet of paper that looks like a release towards me. I feel exposed with a rapidly expanding shadow descending over my shoulder. I want to leave and relegate the whole thing to a shiver of repulsion in the middle of the night. But something compels me toward the paper.

I look at the distorted reflection of me smiling in the glasses on his head. If I didn't know it was me, I would be frightened. I am also surprised to see how much I look like Lucas.

The Naked Sniper

> If my hands had eyes and a chin,
> I imagine them staring out the window,
> chin on fists, wishing there was more to them than me.

The first shot sounded like a cat in heat or a guitar string that had been wound too tightly and snapped. Even if I had noticed the divot in the sidewalk where the bullet, having passed by my right ear, impacted, I would never imagine I mattered enough to someone for them to try to shoot me.

I had always assumed I would die from some long-term debilitating disease, as my mother had. Some disease that would begin with a simple tremor in my right hand and end with the eventual loss of consciousness and bowel control. I can still see my mother's angry, determined face as she finally succumbed, somehow blaming me for being her sole uninspiring legacy. Whatever the eventual cause of my death, I always imagined it would, ironically enough, start with my hands.

Let me just say I am more or less a hunchback. Not in the Quasimodo sense; more in the being asymmetrical sense. But my hump is simply the beginning of my unattractiveness. I am pale year-round and have a near infinite number of moles, from the one on the top of my head to the three on the bottom of my left foot. My hair is like a Brillo pad glued to my scalp that draws you away from my face, which is dominated by thick glasses and, like my shoulders, is also irregular. I have thin lips that curl down at the edges, perfect for my role as a mid-level city bureaucrat. My head seems to sit on my shoulders, which, due to my hump, lean to the left. With my shirt off, in the dark of my bedroom, my chest resembles a birdcage with a cover tightly tightly wound around it. It slopes inward from my shoulders toward my navel. I will skip over everything below the waist because there is little of interest there to anyone, including me.

But my hands, and my fingers especially, are unusually beautiful. They are long and narrow and seem to belong to someone with great dexterity. My mother used to spontaneously grab them and hold them up. "Look," she would say with preemptive disappointment, "these are the hands of an artist. These are the hands of a surgeon, a pianist or an architect." While, to her chagrin, I have the hands but not the talent or tenacity to be anything more than what I became, I have to admit my hands are beautiful.

I often lose myself in thought watching my hands perform their daily tasks. Whether they staple, sign, or file, they do it with such a grace and purpose, that surely they could accomplish so much more. But they never complain as they effortlessly shuffle papers in triplicate, sign and initial where indicated and then casually slip a paper clip across the corner as tenderly as a groom places a ring on his bride's finger. If my hands had eyes and a chin, they would stare out the window, chin on fists, wishing there was more to them than me.

The second shot sounded exactly like a .22 caliber bullet zooming over my head and striking the brick wall I happened to be walking by. Jesus, I thought, someone is trying to shoot me. My first thought was, of course, terror. I spun about madly, looking for the source of the shooting. The third shot pierced the grocery bag I was carrying, narrowly missing the quart of milk, but not the oranges that were next to it. The smell of burning fruit wafted upward and, looking skyward, I noticed the glint of the sniper scope on a nearby building, surrounded by a flurry of pigeons.

When the panic set in, I scurried like a squirrel, trying to find a place to hide. But while my mind was clear, it was not particularly helpful, focusing on random images with useless clarity: The chest of pigeon in flight. The reflection of a street sign in a store window. A green mailbox. The spine of a fire escape winding down the side of a building. A green mailbox. The sole of a boot running in the other direction. And a green mailbox. A green mailbox. I threw myself behind the green mailbox.

I looked up at the sniper. It must have startled him to see me staring back through his scope. The rifle barrel rose and disappeared over the ledge of a six-story building across the street.

I thought about finding a policeman and explaining to him that someone was shooting at me. One or two shots may be just the work of a serial killer who had nothing personal against me. But three shots? Obviously he was trying to shoot *me*. But why?

I couldn't think of anyone or any act that would lead to someone taking rifle in hand to shoot me. Why would the police believe me?

Being a city employee, I anticipated the huge amount of paperwork and inconvenience. I was unhurt and he'd probably been scared off. Considering my position, whole with no holes, I shrugged. What was the worst thing that happened to me? I had to throw out three oranges. Knowing my diet, they would have rotted on the kitchen counter eventually. It was one of those odd city life things. Sometimes someone takes it into his or her mind to take a couple of pot shots at you. Why make a federal case of it?

I looked around me, up and down the sidewalk. A woman with short blond hair in her fifties was no more than hundred feet of me. She had stopped and was considering why I was hiding behind a mailbox. I could see my silhouette reflected in her sunglasses. She was deciding if I was insane or imperiled. Either way, when she saw me looking at her she pantomimed looking at her watch and being late for an appointment in the opposite direction.

But she raised a good question. Was I insane or imperiled? Only physical evidence could decide the matter. I began to look for the slugs. The bullets that struck the concrete had ricocheted down the sidewalk and offstage. But the bullet that struck the brick wall gleaned dully in the afternoon sun. Prying it out with the barrel of a pen, I examined the mushroom-shaped piece of lead. Carved on one side, was the barely legible word –tor. I was fairly sure the letter before had been "c," and the full word was "doctor."

If my mother had still been alive, I would have suspected her of being the shooter. If I could find the other bullets I am sure they would have said "pianist" or "architect." None of the bullets would say "business affairs specialist" as the plastic ID card around my neck announced. Or, according to my mother, "just another faceless cog in the wheel of bureaucracy, except this one has a slight hump on his right shoulder."

The slug felt surprisingly familiar in my hand although I had never held a bullet. I decided to make it a keepsake. Reporting the shooting to the police would only mean its loss.

I glanced across the street to make sure there was no muzzle pointing at me. There wasn't. I dusted myself and my dignity off and pocketed the slug.

On my way home, I took a few precautions, such as walking in a slight serpentine path, distinct enough to avoid bullets and vague enough to avoid notice. I took a different bus home than usual, but that had to do with being late rather than cautious. As a fan of cop shows, I knew enough to enter my apartment from the entrance off the alley instead of the front door.

Needless to say, I did not sleep well that night. I found myself in the middle of the night in the middle of bed on top of a mound of soggy sheets. I went to the bathroom to wash my face.

Even without my glasses I could see the irregular contours of my face. Staring at my reflection, I found little sympathy or solidarity, only doubt and loathing. Was it a face you could truly hate? Not really. Unless it was purely for aesthetic reasons.

"Who would want to kill me?" I asked my reflection. Of course, my job never made me any fans. I could think of at least half a dozen people whose papers were horribly out of order who had muttered vague threats. But if they could not get their C-90s in order, they certainly wouldn't have the wherewithal to plot and carry out an assassination.

When I finally fell asleep I dreamt I was carrying a quantity of ball bearings. I don't know why I was carrying them or where I was taking them, but I could feel both the objects heft and coolness. I wanted to put them down, but I didn't think that was allowed. The dream continued until I awoke to the sound of the morning's first check of traffic on my clock radio.

Stretching I found my hands to be sore, gray and smelling of oil. My hands looked alien, and for the first time in my life, unappealing. I quickly ran into the bathroom to thoroughly clean them, finger by finger. At first, the stains would not come off. But eventually with enough soap, hot water and persistence, my hands became pink again. I was late and had to forego shaving and showering to make it to work on time.

The morning was bright and the autumn wind blew out of the west, scattering dry noisy leaves. The whole world felt refreshed and, if I was not off to City Hall, I might have been philosophical. I had, after all, come through a trial by fire and it was not inconceivable that I was a changed man, hopefully for the better. On the bus, I read the Tribune with interest and thought about whistling as I exited the bus on LaSalle Street. Until a bullet whizzed past my left ear, I felt like I didn't have a care in the world.

Damn, he really is trying to kill me, I thought. I swung about like a weathervane in a tornado, trying to find the sniper. He was in the southeast corner of City Hall's green roof, hiding behind an ornamental grass as if he were big-game hunting in the

Serengeti. I didn't have time to consider what animal I resembled as another bullet struck the pavement between my legs and ricocheted into the side of an eastbound bus. The third bullet shattered a planter of yellow and orange mums, not three feet over my head.

I ran up to a policeman, leaning into a patrol car. He was annoyed when I grabbed him by the shoulder. I pointed towards the top of City Hall. "Somebody's shooting at me. I think he is trying to kill me."

"Who?" he said, sounding bored. He was interrupted by the driver's side's rear window shattering. He threw me to the ground while the patrolman in the car screamed into his walkie-talkie.

Sirens and screeching tires shattered the air. The entire block was soon cordoned off with the exception of me, the officer on top of me, and dozens of cops. Eventually, I was carried by two black-uniformed officers to an alcove out of sight of the roof. Five minutes passed. Ten minutes. Eventually, the SWAT team filed out of the building, finding no sniper on the roof. They had rushed past me with determination in their eyes. As they walked out, each one looked down at me crouched in the doorway, sizing up my story and me with distrust and disgust.

The police turned their suspicion to me. They brought me up to a third-floor room with no windows and only three chairs and a wooden table covered by carved graffiti. I was asked to fill up a pad of paper of what I knew. Knowing very little, it took me very little time to complete the task and return the pad to a mute policewoman with an overbite. I was left alone for half an hour with a cup of already cold coffee.

Finally, the door opened and a hand that looked like it belonged to a gorilla grasped the door knob while the owner continued a conversation in the hallway. The little finger on his right hand was missing. There was laughter in the hall and the hairy knuckles (all four of them) rotated the knob back and forth.

Eventually the owner of the hand came in. He was a square, balding man with wide shoulders, stomach and thighs. In the movies, he would have been the jovial cop who wants to be your friend and, if you would just level with him, he can really help you. He was carrying a file in his left hand, perilously close to the sweat stains under his arm. I wondered if the missing finger would result in a lisp.

"Oh…hi…good morn…afternoon, Mr…ah…," he said, consulting the file. "Mr…geez…Lecowizh?"

"It is pronounced Lekowich."

"Right, Leco…may I call you, Ted? I am lousy with names." He offered a "sorry" shrug to which I responded with a "fine with me" nod. "Great," he said, grunting as he dragged the chair along the floor and then dropped himself into it. He scraped the chair closer to the table with screeches that made me shiver. "Brian," he said, holding out his hand with the missing finger.

I shook it, avoiding touching the empty space where his little finger would have been. His hand was wet and hairy. I slid my hand under the table and wiped it on my pants.

Through the open door, a sullen young man sprang in. He was even squatter than Brian. His dark red hair was short and tightly curled like springs. His face was covered with freckles making him look like a ventriloquist's dummy. I half expected him to sit on Brian's lap. He was not smiling. His eyebrows, broad nose and mouth were three parallel lines, none of them promising. His head and neck were the same circumference and disappeared into his shoulders with a ripple of flesh. He was wearing a blue striped shirt and a dark blue tie that was pulled down to the second button. A large pistol was dangling from his belt.

He said nothing to Brian or me. He walked briskly to the table, swiveled the chair around, and sat astride the back, resting his chin on his hands on top of the chair. He stared at me, practicing his laser vision.

"This is Officer Rizza," Brian said, gesturing to the other cop.

Officer Rizza did not blink or even acknowledge there were others in the room. He just glowered expertly.

"So, Ted, crazy day?" Brian said, unfolding a pair of reading glasses that were in his shirt pocket. "It says here that the shooting started yesterday afternoon in the 5800 Block of North Broadway. Any idea of who is shooting at you?"

"No."

Brian shrugged. "I didn't think so. Which brings us to the next question. Why didn't you report it yesterday?"

It was my turn to shrug. "I don't know. Maybe I was scared or hoped that it was a case of mistaken identity."

Officer Rizza, his head still resting on the back of the chair, muttered "Which is it? You were scared or you thought somebody thought you were someone else?"

"I don't know. I really don't. I just didn't want to make a big deal of it."

"But now it is a big deal, Ted. He's shooting from the top of City Hall. City Hall, Ted. It doesn't get to be a bigger deal than this. I got the mayor's office on my back, understand? And I have to tell them something that makes sense. And I need you to give that to me, because I can't figure it out. Look, I can understand you were scared and maybe hoped that it was all some mix up. But not calling the police? That doesn't make any sense."

"No sense at all," Officer Rizza echoed.

"So if you can help me out here, Ted," Brian continued, flipping through the papers in the file as if he, too, were searching for the answers. "We have only three questions to answer. One, who is shooting at you? Two, why is he shooting at you? And, three, why don't you want us to know about it?"

My head was pounding to the point when a bullet would have been welcome. "I didn't say I don't want you to know about it. Today's different. Now I am sure he is. I would have come in even if one of your officers hadn't sat on me."

Officer Rizza grunted, but didn't say anything. He began to crack his knuckles, loudly, sounding like an animal gnawing on a bone.

Brian looked concerned. "Someone shoots at you and what do you do? You go home and go to bed? It just doesn't make sense. Look, I'm no writer, but I know every story has a beginning, a middle and an end. This one is missing the middle. And in your case, the middle is the most important part."

"I didn't want to get involved if he wasn't trying to kill me. Happy? Isn't that what you wanted to hear? If it wasn't me, why get involved?"

Officer Rizza grunted and pounded his fist like a hoof, which caused everything on the table to jump an inch up. He kept his fist on the table, ready to either pound again or hit me. "Good thing we get involved even when it doesn't concern us. Thank God we are here. Day and night. 24/7. 365 days a week. Serving and protecting. Because without us, you know what would happen? Chaos. Absolute friggin' chaos." He was turning redder and more and more freckles appeared on his face and neck. "Anybody can do anything. And you can't be bothered to call us unless you are sure he is shooting at you. Jesus Christ, if that isn't the most pathetic thing I have ever heard." He fingered the snap on his holster. "I swear to God, I understand why somebody would want to blow your friggin' head off." He pulled himself up by his fists and loomed menacingly over me. "You know who gets shot at? Presidents and drug king pins. Who are you? A nobody! A nobody!" His voice cracked as he yelled.

Brian stood up and put an arm around Officer Rizza to calm him down. Even if it was theater for my benefit, it was pretty convincing. Brian whispered something to Officer Rizza who eventually became less flushed and less animated. Officer Rizza sat down, stared at me and waved his goat-like hand in my direction. "How do you know this isn't some sort of dream?"

"What is? That I am being shot at?" I sighed. "I am not sure it isn't."

"Or a nightmare," he suggested, and for the first time smiled at me.

I sighed again. "A dream. A nightmare. What's the difference?"

"What the fuck does that mean? Jesus Christ," he banged on the table again, "you don't know the difference between a dream and a nightmare?"

"I didn't say that. They're the same to me."

"Oh, for Christ's sake! What kind of crap is that? A dream is something good like a woman with big boobs. A nightmare is something bad, like me pounding you."

I was not trying to be difficult, but he was wrong. "Not for me. If I dream about things I want, I know I will never get them. So it turns out to be a nightmare in the end."

"You want to know what a nightmare is?" Officer Rizza said, standing suddenly and shooting his chair across the room with his thick thighs. "I'll tell you what a nightmare is. Cops getting shot at. Cops getting shot at because of a piece of garbage like you." He stood in front of me with fists clenched. I closed my eyes waiting to be hit.

Instead Brian pushed Officer Rizza out of the room and told him to get a cup of coffee or something. When he turned to face me, he gave me a weak smile and a shrug.

"Please don't blame him. Officer Rizza gets frustrated when he can't figure something out. And, boy, this is a lulu. Look at it from his perspective."

"Why?" I said. "I am the one being shot at."

"And you have no idea why."

"No, I know I have no idea why."

Brian came over and laid his hand on my right shoulder. His missing finger unnerved me. I shrugged it off; I hate it when people touch my hump. He did not seem to be insulted in the least. "Ted, think harder. People don't shoot at other people without a reason. Please think about it a bit harder. According to your file," he said flipping through the papers, "you work upstairs in business affairs. Not a place to make many friends, I imagine."

I shrugged.

"You say no to people each day. You threaten their business. If you did that to me, I might want to kill you."

I did not feel so comfortable with him standing behind me unwatched. I tried to think, but nothing came to mind. Simply, nobody stood out for me. "Sorry, I can't."

The door from the hall flew open and Officer Rizza bolted into the room with his gun drawn. He slammed the pistol on to the table. "Listen, you son of bitch! People don't shoot people for no reason. And they don't shoot nobodies either. You are not telling us something. If you are covering up something, so help me God!" He didn't follow up on that thought.

I don't usually get angry, mostly because I am incapable of intimidating anyone. The best I can usually muster is to mutter under my breath at the legions of people who annoy me. But I was tired, scared and late for work. "Listen, I'm the one he's trying to kill," I shouted back at Officer Rizza.

I thought he would be angry, but he smiled for the first time. "How do you know he's a he?"

"Oh for God's sake! Stop trying to trip me up! I'm guessing he's a he because there hasn't been a she in my life since my mother died. Happy?"

Officer Rizza pursed his lower lip and shrugged. "Not about me being happy."

"All I know is that since yesterday afternoon, someone has been trying to shoot me."

"And you have no idea of who?" Brian asked from his chair.

"Outside of my mother, no?"

"I thought you said she was dead," Officer Rizza said, pushing his nose close to mine.

"She is."

"Then why the fuck did you say she wanted to kill you?"

My face was damp with Officer's Rizza's tobacco-flavored phlegm. "Because I could have sworn one of the bullets had 'doctor' written on it." I reached into my pocket and withdrew the slug that I had hoped to drop off at a jeweler to make into a good luck charm.

"Gimme that," Officer Rizza said. He had the bullet faster than I could give it to him. Brian and he examined the bullet closely, taking turns bringing to the eye and rotating. "Where does it say doctor?" Office Rizza demanded, and slid the slug across the table, expecting me to catch it.

I didn't. I picked it off the floor and showed them the scrawled "-tor." "There, see it? And I think that is a 'c.'"

Officer Rizza examined the slug again. "Where," he asked, nearly snorting it.

"There," I said, pointing.

"You're fucked. That's from the rifling."

I shrugged. "It looked like 'tor' to me. So I figured it spelled doctor. Just trying to be helpful."

"Don't try so hard next time," Officer Rizza said. "I'll take this to the lab and see if matches the slugs we got from the patrol car. But I doubt it will be much help since you pawed it." He left the room without saying anything.

Brian sighed, collected his papers and returned them to file. He stood up and held out his hand. "Thank you for your help, Ted. A piece of advice; I would avoid your usual route home tonight. Maybe you could stay with a family member or a friend."

"I'll be fine."

He shrugged. "Just trying to be helpful. We'll call you if we need you. Good luck."

"Thanks."

Brian nodded and left without saying anything else.

Halfway to my office, I realized that I did not get a note from the police explaining why I was late. There was sure to be hell to pay with Ms. Davis who enjoyed torturing the tardy.

Lucky for me my morning activities were all over the office when I got in. People would look at me with anxious glances and mouth "are you alright?" But no one wanted to get too close to me for fear of errant bullets.

The rest of the day was blissfully quiet. Even the customers heard of the assassination attempt and most of them were willing to wait extra long for another counselor. By the time I left that night, my desk never looked cleaner. If the assassin hit his mark that evening, my replacement would bless my memory.

Ignoring Brian's recommendation, I altered nothing about my commute home. I don't know if it was a death wish or simply to prove that I was somebody. Officer Rizza was right, only important people are targets of assassination attempts. I pondered the possible reasons on my walk down Clark Street. Nothing came to mind, but that did not stop me from feeling exceptional.

That night I had another vivid dream. This time I was walking down an unrecognizable street when there was the whisper of a silenced rifle and the puff of a bullet rushed past my cheek and struck a few inches from left foot. Unafraid, I casually looked to the top of a thirteen-story brick building across the street. I clearly saw the glint of the sniper scope in the afternoon sun and the exhalation of the barrel as another bullet sped towards me. It passed over my right shoulder and shattered the window of a watch repair shop.

I calmly walked into the building, across the Mediterranean-themed lobby with fanciful Greek landscapes painted on the walls. There were two elevators with the number of the floors indicated by a rococo iron pointer. One elevator was open and waiting for me. The other was all the way up on the thirteenth floor. I walked through the open door and pressed thirteen.

Arriving at the thirteenth floor, the door slid opened without apprehension. The other elevator was there, empty, and waiting. I walked out into the hallway. Although I was sure I had never been in this building, it seemed familiar to me. I walked to the end of the corridor and opened the door marked: Roof.

The bright sunlight temporarily blinded me as I exited onto the roof so I did not see the muzzle flash. I did, however, feel the rush of the bullet as it flew past me and struck the Exit sign above my head, glass, like snow flakes, twinkled on my head. Shaking the shards from hair, I waited until my eyes adjusted.

By the low wall, I saw him: the sniper. Actually, what I saw was an enormous eye staring at me through the scope as if I was looking through a peephole. I heard the bolt being pulled back to insert another bullet into chamber.

"Excuse me," I said, "excuse me."

The eye pulled away from the scope and I saw an extraordinarily handsome face. His hair was blonde, of course. Not straw blond but the color of a fine brandy. His face was long and his nose was straight. Had he not been pointing a rifle at my head, I would even say his face had a look of concern. About his neck was a powder blue kerchief. The hands that held the rifle sported the most wondrous fingers I had ever seen. They were lean and muscular and topped off by elegantly trimmed nails with symmetric lunula like so many moons setting on tropical seas. He resembled one of those innumerable British movie stars from the sixties who either played spies or swingers.

When he spoke, he had the accent reserved for the extremely good looking and confident. "Yes?"

"You're shooting at me."

"Pardon?"

"I said, you are shooting at me."

He looked down at the gun, with his right index finger on the trigger. "It would appear so."

"Can I ask you why?"

"Most certainly, although I am afraid you won't like the answer."

"Try me."

"Purely business, nothing personal."

"Business as in someone is paying you?"

He nodded and flashed a wry smile. "Not much call for pro bono services in my line of work I'm afraid."

"So who is paying you?"

Again the smile. "I'm sorry, old chap, purely confidential. I am sure you understand."

And in the dream, I did. But it was worth a chance. "Is it my mother?"

"Sorry, confidentiality extends beyond the grave."

I started to walk away, but stopped and turned around. He was fishing some additional shells from the pocket of his houndstooth jacket. "Can I ask you one more question?"

He aimed the rifle directly at my forehead and pulled the trigger. There was the sound of the hammer clicking in the empty chamber. "It appears so," he said, pulling the bolt back.

"So if you are such a professional, why do you keep missing me?"

Again, he pointed the rifle again, but did not pull the trigger. "I am giving you time to repent."

"Repent for what?"

"Again that would be a breech of confidentiality." He stared at me as the devout regard a heretic. "And if you really don't know why you have cause to repent, it is fortunate I am giving you more time to consider it, isn't it? I do have to confess that it is also a bit of lark for me as well." He smiled again and said, "That part is completely gratis."

"Gee, thanks."

"Do not mention it." He wiped the barrel with a cloth.

I turned around and walked toward the door. A shot rang out and smacked into the wall directly above my head. I spun around.

He flashed a perfect smile. "Whee."

In the morning I woke up with sore hands the color of rain clouds and an overwhelming sense of guilt. As I shaved, showered and ate breakfast, nothing came to mind which could only mean a repressed memory or that I was callous.

Leaving my apartment building, I was assaulted by an angry rainstorm and the wind howling into my face as if Nature, herself, had joined the conspiracy against me. Malevolent raindrops slammed into me turning my umbrella inside out. By the time I made it to the bus stop, I was completely soaked.

When the automatic voice announced my stop, the rain had ended and the sky was simply gray. Exiting the bus, another bullet sailed passed me and ricocheted off the column of a building I was passing. If anyone else noticed, they didn't seem to acknowledge it. But I did.

Looking across the street, I saw the flash of the muzzle and didn't know where the bullet landed as I was dodging traffic, running into the building. I had had enough. If he wanted to kill me, I gave him as large a target as possible.

The building was unfamiliar. The lobby was dark and covered in the greasy marble favored by mausoleums and bus station restrooms. I waited for the elevator, trying to catch my breath. Finally, the elevator came and I had to wait until it emptied. By that time, five other people joined me in the elevator and, of course, were going to different floors.

There was no obvious door to the roof. I walked up and down the hallway twice, even scanning the ceiling for an opening. Figuring he was long gone, I had just pushed the down button when I noticed the janitor's closet door was slightly open and felt a cool breeze coming from it.

I opened the door and saw a metal ladder leading up to the roof. At the base of the ladder was a puddle and pigeon feathers. Without a thought to my safety, I scrambled up the ladder.

I expected the roof to be deserted when I arrived at the top. I saw the back of a man madly pulling something in front of him. He was wearing a long-sleeved undershirt and filthy grey trousers held up by red and white suspenders. As if this was not strange enough he wore a battered helmet similar to those the Nazis wore. The helmet was speckled with white splotches resembling bird shit.

He was unaware of me as I walked across the roof. He kept pulling something with his right arm while his left arm held it steady as if he were trying to start a reluctant chainsaw. He was muttering to himself in some language that sounded like he was trying to clear his throat.

I looked about for some sort of weapon, but only found an old umbrella that must have been blown up there during the storm. The ribs had been bent in several directions and it looked more like a crushed spider than anything else. I gripped it at several places to determine which way made it seem more menacing. But there is only so much that one can do to with a broken umbrella and its most threatening quality was the question: who would be crazy enough to use it as a weapon?

I held it in front of me and came up behind the twitching figure, ready to strike at any provocation with as much force and dignity that the situation would allow.

Standing behind him, I faced a moral dilemma. Despite the fact he had spent the better part of two days trying to shoot me from a hidden position, it seemed underhanded to hit him unawares.

Keeping the umbrella in my right hand, I tapped him on the shoulder with my left. "Excuse me."

He shot straight up, with his hands in the air. His rifle, which was somehow still attached to him, dangled from his waist, swinging like a pendulum. "Schießen Sie nicht!" he called out.

"Excuse me?"

He turned around and looked at me as if I was the last person he expected to see on the roof. I had the same feeling. I was expecting to find a suave, handsome Englishman, but was faced with a sad face man with a large nose and obvious lumpy central European features. He looked vaguely familiar as if I had seen him in a movie at one time. He pursed his lips and tried to whistle as casually as a man with a rifle dangling from his crotch could be.

"You are shooting at me."

"Ich? Pshaw!" he said, flipping his right hand, striking the rifle, causing it to spin like a propeller. "But I think know you. Where would I see you?"

"Perhaps through your sniper scope." I said, staring at the rifle dangling between his legs.

"I also you have seen in my doorhole." He blanched and put his hands to his mouth to prevent further disclosure.

"Doorhole? What's a doorhole?"

He made a ring with his index finger and thumb and put it up to his eye. There was something peculiar about his fingers; it was as if they were each missing a joint and he had to struggle to make them meet. They reminded me of Vienna sausages; short, plump and gray. "You know, the hole in the door for looking."

"What do you mean? Wait a minute, we'll get to that later. You are shooting at me."

He nodded his head sadly, pursing out his lower lip. "Ja. Ja. And I miss you." He hung his head in shame. "So sorry."

"Sorry? Don't mention it," I said, my voice dripping with sarcasm.

He actually brightened. "Danke. You are so much understanding."

"Can I ask you why you are shooting at me?"

He shrugged. "Just following orders."

"And I don't suppose you can tell me whose orders?"

He brightened up. "It is keine secret. I am following your orders."

Had I heard him right? "Excuse me?"

"Ja. You give me cash money to shoot you." He must have seen the confusion in my face. "I, too, think it is odd that you pay me to kill you and bring me the bullets, too."

"What do you mean I bring you the bullets?"

"Every night, you come to my apartment and bring me a handful of bullets. Two handfuls," he said, illustrating his point by showing two sausage-sized fingers.

"I do?"

"Ja and in your pajamas, too. Very odd, nein?"

"I come to your apartment in my pajamas?"

He nodded enthusiastically. "You give me cash money and many many bullets. More than I can use. Maybe you know I am not so good at shooting." He pouted, looked down his hands and the rifle dangling by his crotch and sighed. "Not very good at all."

I steadied myself on a short wall. "When did you first meet me?"

He put his stubby index finger to his lip and silently counted the days. "Today is Thursday, right? That would mean you came first Monday night or very early Tuesday morning. I was asleep when you knocked. Knocked very loud and very much." He used his helmet to demonstrate how I knocked on his door. "I was very frightened and did not want to let you in."

"Why did you?"

"You knew my name. 'Let me in Franz Liebkind or I will tell authorities all I know.'"

"So you're Franz Liebkind?"

"Quiet, please!" he waved a hand at me like he was fanning flames. "Do not play your jokes on me. It is bad enough that you came here."

"Okay, so I knew your name. It was probably written on your mailbox."

He looked insulted. "I tells people mein name is Freddy Lovechild. That is why I was so frightened. You knew my real name. Who knows what else you know about me? You were pounding so hard, I am afraid you would wake the neighbors and so I let you in."

"So I came in and what do I say to you?"

"You don't know? Or are you playing with me again?"

"I'm playing with you? You're the one shooting at me!"

He looked insulted. "At your orders." He crossed his arms and tried to assume as much dignity as was possible.

"Look, I'm sorry. I am just as confused as you are. Believe me. I am."

He looked unconvinced.

"What did I tell you?"

"You came in, told me you wanted me to kill someone. I told you I didn't know what you were talking about, but you kept staring at me without saying nothing. So I told you it would cost you $1,000. You shook your head and told me that was too much. You said you would give me $250 and would supply the bullets. You told me that you knew I needed the money. How did you know I needed the money? I was…how you say…frechted out? You handed me a picture and told me you wanted me to shoot the man in the picture. And then you frechted me out even more. I looked at the picture and it was you. 'But this is you,' I said. You nodded and handed me a piece of paper on which was written your address, your place of work, and the way you go between them. You handed me a handful of bullets and told me that should be enough. It was like forty bullets. Finally you gave me an envelope in which was $125. You told me I would get the other half when the job was done."

"Why didn't you just report me to the police?"

"You told me not to."

"And you listened to me?"

"You were very convincing. You seemed to know so much about me that I figured the only way to be really safe was to take your money and kill you. I said you must be a very sad man if you wanted someone to kill you. You told me not to feel sorry for you. You said you deserved to die. And you told me that you would see me tomorrow. And you laughed and told me that it was actually I who would see you tomorrow. And you made this kind of gun with you fingers and pointed at me. It was very scary. And then you left."

"And so I tried to shoot you as you walked home. I was already with my rifle, bullets and a little something to eat. I always get hungry when I am nervous. You got off the bus and were walking very slowly. I took a deep breath, aimed and missed. I shoot again and missed again. And a third time. And then you hide behind mailbox and I do not see you any more. I thought that was the last I would see of you."

"But that night. Late at night. You knock on my door again. Loud. I didn't want to let you in, but I knew you would not go away. I open the door and there you were again. Still in your pajamas. And with more bullets. When you had to know I still had so viel bullets left! And then what do you do the next day? I shoot and shoot at you when there are so many police around that I almost was caught. And what do you do? You come last night to mein apartment with…what…more bullets! Why do you torture me?" He dropped his chin into his chest and stared at the rifle in disgust.

It was a pathetic sight for which I felt partially responsible. I put my hand on his shoulder and he flinched as if I was about to punch him. "Look, I am sorry I made you feel bad."

He shook his head slowly. "No, it is my fault. I am paying for the sins of mein youth. I see you, I put the crosshair on your head, and then a little voice tells me I am not good at shooting. I squeeze the trigger and I miss. I am an incompetent. A total incompetent." He dropped his head and began to sniffle again.

"It is these hands," he said, holding his stubby fingers up. What are they good for? Absolutely nothing! Garnicht!"

The image in front of me was pathetic. "Look," I said, "I have a great idea. Why don't you stop shooting me? I won't say anything."

He looked up with a face full of tears. "Nein, danke, you will know and I will know. What would be the point?"

He shook his head. He grabbed and pulled on the stock and he eventually ripped his shirt. For a moment, I thought he was going to shoot me, but he took the rifle and put the muzzle under his chin. He managed to loop his thick thumb on the trigger. I closed my eyes and waited for the bang. But all I heard was the sound of the rifle clattering on the roof. Apparently there was still a piece of his shirt in the chamber. "You see, you see? I can't even kill myself." He picked up the rifle, pulled the trigger and a shot went off. A passing pigeon exploded above us and spiraled down to the street. He sighed and looked over the edge of the roof as if the pigeon was staring up at him in pity.

Although he was trying to kill me, I felt guilty. But what could I do? And then it hit me.

"Mr. Liebkind, listen to me. Stop crying and listen to me." I raised my umbrella over my head like a riding crop.

He cringed and wailed "Why must you torture me? You are so cruel! Sometimes I think you are mein worst nightmare."

"I know the feeling," I said, watching him collapsing by the low wall that circled the roof. His rifle lay on the ground by my feet. He put his head in his hands and wept. I could have easily picked up and either arrested or shot him.

I am not one for inspiration, but the stew that usually sloshes through my mind parted and I had a clear view of the way out. I straightened myself as best as my warped shoulder would allow and shouted: "Liebkind, you maggot, stop crying and stand up. Now!"

Rousing whatever dignity he could muster, he dusted himself off and stood up. "Jawohl!" He was at attention with his rifle tucked against his right side. "Now listen to me," I said. "Stop sniveling."

He wiped his moist nose with his left hand and looked straight ahead.

"Are you listening?"

"Jawohl!" He nodded, his helmet falling across his eyes, but he left it there.

"I cancel my previous order. You are to stop trying to kill me. Do you understand? Cease and desist. Understand?"

"Jawohl!"

"Now, I want you to stop feeling like a failure, because shooting me would be in direct violation of my orders. Do you understand?"

"Jawohl!"

"And what do you understand?"

"That I am not to shoot you."

"And are you a loser?"

"Nein, mein herr!"

"At ease," I said, dropping the umbrella to the ground. Having done my good deed for the day, I turned around and began to walk to the hole in the roof. A shot rang out and ricocheted off the top of the metal ladder.

I spun around and stared at him. The smoke was still streaming out of the muzzle. He cursed quietly.

"What the hell?" I asked. "I ordered you to stop shooting at me."

"You did, mein Herr, but last night you ordered me to ignore all other orders." He put the rifle up to his face and I could see his eye magnified in the scope. I watched his finger tightened on trigger and swore I could see the bullet leaving the muzzle. The bullet whizzed past my left cheek and sailed into the sky.

"Scheis!" he swore, reaching into his pocket for more bullets. They fell all over the roof, of course. I began to walk away shaking my head. He smiled at me as if he knew something I did not. "See you tomorrow," he said waving his stubby hand.

"See you tonight," I said. The confidence drained from his face as he searched his pockets in vain.

I headed for the ladder, but stopped and looked back at him. "Fritz, just curious, did I tell you what I did to deserve to die?"

"No. You said it wasn't for something you did, but something you did not do."

I nodded sadly and began to climb down the ladder. I hoped the tremors in my right hand would quiet once my heart stopped pounding.

A Stone's Throw

Lather Rinse Repeat

Naomi is tired and the kids are on her nerves. She says, let's go to Lighthouse Beach. I say all right, though I'm tired, too. Working at Frankie's all day really wears me out. I'm learning as fast as I can to be a mechanic. Most of the time, I'm just doing oil changes, moving cars around the lot or filling the candy machine. Three nights a week, I'm at Central Maine, studying automotive repair. It's nearly two hours each way. All this running makes me real tired. So tired that maybe I just want to stay at home and watch a Sox game and drink a beer or three.

    Naomi don't take no for answer. She looks at Russell, my ten-year-old, who is supposed to live with us half the week, but is with us most of the time because his mother, Karen, is a drunk and a whore. Naomi says Russell's got his mother's wildness because he likes to burn things and mess with animals he's caught in the woods. She says she's the one raising Russell, not Karen, not me. A boy like that can wear you out real fast. Charlotte, who's hers and mine, is seven but looks and acts like she is four. She's a sweet enough girl, but she's not all there. Raising kids and cleaning houses makes Naomi tired. Tired and mean.

    We get in the Maverick and drive out of town toward the Owl's Head Light. For any other car it's a fifteen-minute drive. But the Maverick only has three working cylinders and needs a new radiator. It's hot and the car's hot, too. It can only go so far before

I need to pull over and let the engine cool. Naomi gets hot when the car gets hot and she asks me again when am I going to fix the damn thing. I tell her I'm working on it. Which I'm not. Because it's real hard to find a radiator for a '76 Maverick and, even if I did, how'm I going to pay for it?

. . .

In college, my roommates and I and our girlfriends would drive up from Massachusetts, buy beer in New Hampshire, and spend three nights in Bangor, one in Augusta and two in Portland at Dead shows. In my memories Maine is a magical place full of tradition, loose women and easy-to-obtain drugs. A Shangri-La for liberal arts college students. Of course, I was heavily self-medicated, so some of my Maine reminiscences may be mere memories of hallucinations.

But I can't forget waking up, the car windows frosted by nighttime activity, and staggering into the moist woods to take a leak. I stumbled into a small family cemetery, taking a leak on a grave from boy who was lost at sea in 1822 when he was seventeen. Talk about consciousness, crystal-clear autumn morning clarity: me, my place in the universe and the meaning of it all. I drew in the morning air, cold and wet, and I could feel it cooling my blood. I was nineteen, hungover and understood everything.

And then I am thirty-nine with a wife and two kids. A job that is far less than anything I could have anticipated when I was in college. Back then, the world was full of options from novelist to lobsterman. But now our mortgage makes the very ground under my feet seem capricious and unstable and precludes nothing but the most practical career. I wake up in the morning wishing for good luck and go to bed disappointed.

In college the world was only limited by the width of the horizon. Now it seems as big as a closet with all the crap I've accumulated in my life stuffed inside to keep me company. I haven't been stoned in years and the last time I got drunk, I threw up and nearly flushed my cell phone down the toilet. Seven hundred bucks later I squirmed uncomfortably in the presence of the twenty-something plumber who knows all too well what happens and pities me my lost years.

Some time in my early thirties, I forgot about Maine. My last Dead tour t-shirt stopped being a rag at least fifteen years ago and was thrown out, lemony-Pledge fresh. The rest of Maine was stuffed in a box up in the attic, waiting to be left out for Purple Heart.

My wife, Sara, told me we needed something more than just weekend trips this summer. The girls, Haley and Olivia, five and three respectively, were getting older and next year we would be too involved with summer camp to go on a vacation longer than a couple of days. I seemed more neurotic than normal and could use some time to rest my pessimism muscles. She looked at our Google calendars and found a two-week period that was populated with moveable meetings and missable obligations.

She found a cabin on a small island about ten miles south of Rockland, Maine. It seemed built for the four of us, overlooking a small bay. A place the world, and its problems, couldn't find us. She told me the water wasn't potable as if that were a positive. And, she added, glowering at our twin Blackberries contently recharging on the counter, she was pretty sure the cell phone service would be minimal or nonexistent. Before I could complain that I had a lot of projects due in early September, she told me she had purchased non-refundable plane tickets. Besides, she said, there are a lot of lighthouses, maybe one of them hiring.

. . .

The Maverick hates gravel roads. It never had great traction, but with a sticky ball joint, it's like driving in pudding. Even on flat roads, it bounces around. I have to fix that too, along with the passenger door. Damn thing hasn't opened in years. But when we hit the pothole at the park entrance, I am pretty sure the tie rod has broken and the axle bent.

Naomi looks at me with that look of hers and tells me not to put another dime into the car. Not half an hour ago she was yelling at me to fix it. Fine with me. How'm I going to get to work or school? How we gonna get groceries or go to the park if we don't have a car?

The tire didn't fall off. But I park close to the road. I'm taking no chance of not making it back onto Shore Drive. I move the spare tire that's flat and we take out the bag with the towels and the box with sandwiches from Togos out of the trunk. Naomi takes out the juice boxes and I take out the soda. I would love a beer, but the last time we were here a cop caught us and told he would let us go, but he would be watching us. I can't afford any more trouble. It always seems to find me. It's got my number, my address, and my stones.

I almost tripped on Charlotte. She's standing right in front of me. She wants me to carry her. I tell her no. My arms are full. She can walk. But she sits on the ground. Charlotte is tough like her mother. She likes to get in the way. One day she'll learn that most people will just run her over. I got tire marks on my back.

I have a headache and I'm tired. When do I get a break? I push her with my foot. I watch Naomi to make sure she isn't watching. She hates when I get mad. She asks me why I get mad. Why do I get mad? Maybe because my life sucks? Maybe I just want some luck, without the word "bad" in front of it?

Charlotte is screaming. I am pushing her with my foot, dragging her butt on the gravel. She says it hurts. I tell her to get up. She says no. Man, I want to kick her ass from here to China. But she'll get her way. All she has to do is cry or even look sad and Naomi kicks my ass. She tells me to pick Charlotte up and carry her on my shoulder. I am carrying the towels and the lunches and now she wants me to carry Charlotte.

My right shoulder hurts like a bitch with her on it. It's been hurting for over a week. I was trying to get a rusted lug nut off of the tire of a F-150. I had to put all my weight on the wrench. I heard a snap and thought the stud broke. But all of a sudden I saw black and it felt like someone had ripped my arm off. I put ice on it and popped like half a bottle of aspirin until my stomach burned. Naomi told me to go to the clinic. But I hate that place. Full of coughing and whining people. What were they going to say? Take some time off? Wear a brace? That's not going to happen. Eventually it's gonna hurt less or I'll get used to it.

"House," Charlotte says, grinding her hips into my shoulder. She's trying to drive me with her knees. "I wanna go to the house."

There are two paths, one down to the water, one up to the lighthouse. "I'm not going up to the lighthouse. There's nothing to see up there," I lie. It's a beautiful day and when I was Charlotte's age, I used to love to run up the stairs to the bluff. Up there you can see across the harbor to Rockland, and on a day like this, all the way up to Rockport or even Camden. Back then, I thought I could do more than look. I thought I could run away.

But I'm not a kid anymore and hate the idea of walking all the way up to the lighthouse and back down to the ocean. My shoulder is killing me and my feet hurt. I could use new sneakers. All I want to do is get into the water and float in the cold water.

"House," Charlotte is screaming in my ear. I try real hard not to throw her off. Just shut up already. Naomi, who's telling Russell to stop dragging his feet, tells me to stop thinking about myself. Like I ever get a chance to think about me.

My back aches by the time we get to the top. Charlotte points at the boats in the harbor and laughs. Russell throws rocks at the seagulls. I put Charlotte down so she can play with the small statue of a girl the keepers put up to collect change for widows and orphans. She always talks to the girl and makes sure that Russell doesn't steal the change when no one is looking. I rub my shoulder and my back. I can't even stand straight anymore. Either I am bent under a car or I am in those hard seats with the attached desk at the college.

The wind is blowing and the sun is shining. It's a nice day. I watch a couple with their two little girls climb up the stairs. I can tell they're from away. They're tourists who make the coast crowded from June to September. I turn and look at the harbor. I know what they will think when they make it up here. It is perfect. The water. The sun. The boats. I've heard it all before. They want to quit their jobs and live here.

They must think that we all have water views and spend the afternoons on our boats. The only view I get is my neighbors' cracked bathroom window. They don't know and never will know the Maine after September. When it gets gray and everything just slows down and freezes and the grocery store keeps trying to sell you the same limp celery and brown apples because they're too cheap to throw them out.

Take a walk in my sneakers for a couple of days and tell me it is so damn wonderful here. I would love to move to Boston or New York or Phoenix—wherever they live. I would give up the sun, the water, and the boats not to feel the load on my back.

"Down," Charlotte says. She wants to go swimming. I don't say anything because no one is listening. I pick her up and the towels and lunch and down the stairs and the path that we just came up. We have to walk almost back to the parking lot to take the path down to the water.

We pass the family on the way up the stairs. They are oohing and ahhing and taking like a thousand pictures. I hate them and their easy life.

. . .

The guy we passed looked like Charles Manson and I look like just the type of guy old Charlie would like to take for a short walk into the woods with a long knife.

I made sure to keep the girls in front of me with myself between them and Manson. Haley was out of her mind with excitement. I bought her a small digital camera and she completely filled the memory card with pictures of the car, the gravel road, trees, the sky, and the Manson family.

Haley held up the camera and told me, "Fiss it." The memory card was full and I started to deleting pictures: our rental car, gravel, sky, and trees. The final picture was of the Charlie Manson. It was a picture of his head, cut off at the forehead. His eyes were dark and sunken. A stiff breeze could have knocked him over. He was probably somewhere in his twenties; his face probably cleared up finally only a couple of weeks ago and was now framed by a wispy beard. But he looked like he would skip his thirties and go right to being old. He was looking right at the camera—or more likely through it—with a combination of hate and apathy. Even after deleting the picture, I could see his eyes. They were the type of eyes that would visit you at night in the darkened halls of your house.

I shivered and glanced over my shoulder as I walked up the stairs toward the Lighthouse. Our eyes met and I looked down. What was he thinking? Was he plotting to follow me, waiting to get me alone in the shadow of the lighthouse? I caught up to the girls and only when I had the hill between the two of us did I dare take another look. He was at the base of the stairs, looking up. From this distance, I couldn't tell if he was looking at me. He disappeared into the woods down the path heading down toward the water.

The sun was warm and the breeze caressed our cheeks. The view was spectacular; the ocean was deep blue, the sky azure and the sails on the boats, bleached white. But I couldn't enjoy the view. Sara saw me gnawing on my lower lip. She asked me why can't you ever enjoy the view instead of worrying about what is around the next corner. I nodded noncommittally, but all I could think about was him waiting for us to come down. How did I know he wasn't waiting for me by the car? They were probably a family of thieves. Each would take out one of us with knives of diminishing size. Would the police find our bodies before the snow came? I felt nauseated and didn't hear Olivia when she told me she wanted to go down to the beach. When I finally heard her, I told her no.

My excuses were lame: The water was cold. The beach was rocky. Look at the boats. Aren't they pretty? Why would we want to go anyplace else? Sara told me to stop being boring. Wasn't I the one who said there was nothing to see up here in the first place? She said, we came here to relax, so relax. Easy for her to say. She didn't notice the Manson family.

But three disappointed stares told me that I had no choice. The girls took off down the path toward the bay. Sara wanted to zip her fingers into mine, but I was not in the mood for a romantic walk down the water. Not while there was a homicidal maniac waiting for my daughters just around the bend in the path. I started to walk fast, letting gravity and anxiety drive me forward. The best that Sara could do was to follow behind, trying to hook my belt loop with her finger. I kept all my attention fixed on Haley's ponytail as it bobbed up and down. So long as I could see it, nothing bad was happening.

The woods opened up on to a picture-perfect panorama of pines, granite, skies, and silky seas. I stopped and Sara careened into my back. I scanned the beach wildly for the girls. They were to my left trying to climb a granite boulder by the water, causing

Sara concern and she ran down the beach to make sure they didn't fall into the surf.

But I was temporarily relieved as the Mansons were on the other side of the beach, directly under the hill that we had just come down. They were in the process of stripping out of their clothes, the younger girl in a tight bathing suit decorated with faded images of obscure Disney characters. The boy was wearing gym shorts that weren't technically swim trunks. He was scratching the sand with a stick, searching for clams. When he found them, he would place them on the nearest flat surface to smash them. Lovely.

Charlie Manson was simply wearing the same shorts I had seem him in before. He had taken off his shirt, which probably accounted for half his weight. You could see his bones through his taut skin and floated on his back, probably unable to sink.

. . .

The sun is in my eyes. I don't put my hands over my eyes, because the water feels so good on my sore shoulder. I can hear Charlotte and Naomi splashing by the beach. The ocean just groans. I don't get many times like this. I could just float on my back and let the ocean take me where it like. Out into the harbor, into Penobscot Bay and into the ocean. Let someone else drive for awhile.

Naomi is yelling at Russell. She is saying something that began with "don't" and ended "or else." I am usually the "or else" guy. Russell's gonna be trouble. He probably already is. There's nothing I can do about it. Why would he listen to me? He is just going to have to find his way like I did. So long as you stay out of the way of the guys who are meaner and bigger than you, you'll be fine. That's about all I got and he knows it already.

The water is rocking me to sleep. I know I should wake up. The ocean wants to kill me, but it's the only thing I trust.

I look at Naomi. She's growing tired of going nowhere. We've argue more and more. She'll leave soon. Probably take Charlotte with her and take up with someone else who is no good for her either. They'll have a kid or two and then realize what a mistake they made. I will be lucky if Russell runs away before he's 16. The back door will slam and he'll be gone with the sound of gravel being kicked up. I'm sure I won't be upset just like my old man wasn't when I left.

The guy from the lighthouse is on the beach with his family. They are laughing. Of course they are laughing. What do they have to worry about? Where their kids are going to go to college? What color their new car should be? They're not swimming, but it doesn't matter, they're floating through life.

The mother is up on the beach, shoes off, pants rolled up looking for rocks with the younger girl. I never knew why people from away look for stones. One is just as good as another. But they always spend hours picking up stones. What do they do with them when they get home?

The father is in the water up to his shins. He has the other girl with him, the younger one. He is looking for stones in the water, too. He throws most of them away. He is waving his arm around like he is waving to someone out in the bay. But there is nobody there. Just waving because he can wave. What a life.

. . .

The water felt like ice; I never got used to it. I tried not tiptoe over the stones on the beach. I didn't want Haley to think her father was a wuss. She's not used to stone beaches. To her the beach is sand, buckets, shovels, and about a thousand other people. But other than the Manson family, no one else was around.

My right foot stepped on a flat rock that wedged itself between my toes. I picked it up and held it in my hand. It was flat on both sides and about the same size as a Reese's peanut butter cup. I fling it with a side arm motion. It hopped once, twice, three times in a gentle arc. Haley laughed like she just saw magic.

I remembered standing in a warm Michigan lake in the early seventies. I was about the same age as Haley, maybe a bit older. My father flicked his wrist shooting stones across the water's surface—five, six, or even seven hops before they dove to the bottom. It was the greatest thing I had ever seen—a rock flying through the air. I figured with the right angle they would fly forever.

"Do it again, daddy," Haley screamed, "Do it again. Make the rock fly!" I hate to break it to her that eventually all stones sink. I picked up another rock from beneath my feet. It was flat on one side, but round on the other. Not ideal, but who cares? I pulled my arm back and let it fly. It arced and dove straight down. I plunged my hand into the freezing water again and picked up the first rock I could find. It was more round than flat. I let it fly and it spun as it hit the water and perhaps jumped once before it crashed into a wave and disappeared. Haley sighed.

I grabbed another stone that seemed vaguely appropriate. I drew back my arm and flung it as hard as I could. This one was going to skip or else. Like so many times in my life, "or else" happened. The rock flew out of my hand and never touched the water, instead it smashed into Charlie's face with a thud. He must have floated towards me when I wasn't watching. He was no more than 30 feet away when the rock hit him. I could see him grabbing his mouth with both hand and the blood mixing with water running down his chest.

. . .

I see the rock coming at me. It's traveling really slow, but I can't get out of the way. It hits me right in the mouth and I hear two teeth crack.

The guy is over before I know it. He's sorry. He didn't see me. He's shaking and asks if he could take me to the hospital. What can they do? Fix my teeth? I spit blood and tell him I'm fine. He follows me out of the water like he's afraid I'm gonna faint or something. It isn't like the first time I got hurt. It probably isn't going to be the last. I tell him to leave me alone. I'll be fine. I walk past Naomi and Russell, who is smiling at me. He thinks it's cool. I need a beer and some ice. But all we have is a warm can of Hannaford's Root Beer.

. . .

I didn't know what else to do so I gave his girlfriend my business card and told her to call me if I could be help. Sara came over with Olivia and whispered to me that I was nuts to give them my number. They'll sue us. She was probably right. I wasn't thinking. Then to make it even worse, I asked for their number and told her I would call that night to see how things went. I watched them pack up their things, kids crying, lunches thrown into the bushes, walking slowly back to their car. He had the little girl on his shoulder, kicking him as he walked. The vacation ruined, we headed back into town while the girls complained that Maine smelled like fish but I thought it smelled of an impending lawsuit.

Of course I didn't call. I figured I would call them when we got home so I wouldn't have to see them again. But I was very busy when I got home. The stress hit me when I pulled into the parking garage. I became basically unbearable when I saw the pile of mail in my inbox and the phone's insistent flashing that told me my voicemail was nearly full. But it gave me an excuse not to call them and I was relieved. A week went by. And then two. I was wondering how long it would be before I stopped thinking about it so I could claim absentmindedness.

A month later, I was paying for a client lunch when I saw their number on my business card; the saltwater made it curly like a lasagna noodle. I promised to call when I got home to see how they were doing. But I didn't and another month passed and with it came the welcome feeling that calling now would only make me looking insensitive. They didn't call me, so everything must be all right, right?

But sometimes when I was helping Olivia brush her teeth or eating a chocolate chip cookie and biting into a walnut shell, I remembered and shivered. I saw the stone leaving my hand and flying towards his face. I saw it hit his mouth and the blood was everywhere. It was like a car accident, repeating over and over again. Why hadn't I called? What must they think of me? I went through my wallet only to find that I had lost the card. I took everything out twice; but it was gone.

I told Sara I had a bad feeling about Charlie. She hated my feelings because they always had two components—one, being dark and dank and two, being wrong, which made me only think of something worse. I was sure he was busily decomposing sans two front teeth. Or did they put his teeth in with him before they shut the coffin?

I had never obsessed about teeth, but now I couldn't help it. I stared at people's incisors as they talked or ate. I stared at my canines in the mirror, running my tongue along their pointed surfaces. I was like a vampire, not only literally sucking the life of Charlie Manson, but sucking the joy out of everyone around me, until Sara told me to get some help. On the break room wall was a poster from our employee assistance program offering a safe and confidential person to talk to.

The call was formulaic. A woman with a confident and conciliatory voice told me to be fair to myself. It had been an accident. I didn't mean to hit him. These things happened and while it was too bad that he had lost a couple of teeth, there are worse things. I said she was probably right, and declined her offer of two more free sessions.

I accepted what my counselor had told me and I worked the story into my repertory at cocktail parties between the second and third drink. I began to embellish the story increasing the size of the rock and the number of teeth he lost and for some reason he developed a southern accent, peppered with blue speech.

I would have forgotten the whole thing if I hadn't put on a sports coat I hadn't worn for a while. In the breast pocket I found the business card with Naomi's number on it.

What the hell, I thought, when I got back to my desk. A woman answered the phone on the third ring. I asked if she was Naomi. No, she said. I asked her if Naomi was there. No, she said. She told me Naomi didn't live there anymore. I asked her if she knew where I could reach Naomi. No, but she wished she did because the landlord is charging her for damage to the walls and she is sure as hell sure that none of her kids did it. I should be sure to tell Naomi to call her if I ever found her. And then, by way of an afterthought, she told me that she heard that Naomi was in Bangor. She went there with her daughter after her boyfriend died.

He died? I asked. How? She said she didn't know. It was almost a year ago. She didn't know him very well. But she heard it was lockjaw or something. He waited too long to get to the doctor.

The air swirled in front of me. I was about to hang up when I remembered the boy. The one crushing clams on the seashore. I asked her if she knew what happened to him.

No, she said, she didn't know what happened to him. Probably got in trouble and was in jail. She was pretty sure he was the one who scuffed up the walls. Served him right. She never liked that boy; too much like his father.

I'm With Stupid

[Illustration: two faces with text "All the voices?"]

Crap, don't turn around. Don't. Shit. If only you had sprung for the Zyrtec instead of insisting on the generic, you would never have seen me. But today you decide it's okay to sneeze like a goddamned Tourette patient. Anybody but you would be too busy sneezing to notice how much you are annoying just about everybody, especially me.

In mid-sneeze, you swivel your head and catch me hand to mouth, whispering in your ear. I am at least four inches taller than you, but leaning over, my mouth is level with your ear. The words "you are annoying peop..." freeze in my mouth.

If anonymity was my goal, I wouldn't have worn my "I'm with Stupid" t-shirt, bright orange cargo shorts, and flip-flops. Add my spiked hair and van-dyke beard and I am pretty much guaranteed to be noticed. Especially in the middle of early

November flurries. But I have hated my job for years and with nothing new on the horizon, I say fuck it. Might as well be comfortable.

Considering I am nearly French kissing your earlobe, I'm not surprised you ask what am I doing.

"You're not supposed to see me," I say, sure the freckles on my nose are lit up like fireworks. There's hell to pay when we get caught. It is a sign of slackness and carelessness. A lecture on professionalism is in my near future.

"What are you doing?" you ask, patting the wallet in your back pocket and the keys in the front. Everything seems in order, except for the fact that you have a complete stranger whispering in your ear. You are wondering how long I have been there, and what do I mean, you are really annoying people? Who the hell am I? And how do I know what you are thinking?

I say nothing, doing my impersonation of a light pole. You try to do that pathetical casual thing of yours. You take maybe twenty steps and turn around quickly, catching me whispering: "Who is he? Is he dangerous? Why is he whispering in my ear? And how does he know I worry about annoying people?"

Next you try to kid yourself that accepting criticism is some sort of vaccine, protecting you from something worse. Wrong. You try to be circumspect. Most people are afraid of annoying others. But you don't have the balls to carry it off. You give in and wonder if it is just you.

Another impromptu sneeze and I am right back in your ear, whispering "Is it just me?"

"Who are you and why are you talking in my ear?"

This isn't part of the deal. But I've been caught. "It's bad enough to have to follow you around all day. Explaining why is not in my job description."

"Your job description?" you ask. "What are you talking about?"

I straighten up and look down at you, trying to intimidate you into ignoring me. You are too spooked to ask any questions, but too fucked up to forget it.

And like matter and antimatter colliding, only bad things can happen when we meet. I am guaranteed to be up half the night filling in forms. Why can't you just accept I am just a guy who whispers unpleasantries in your ear? I am certainly not the first and I won't be the last. I can't say anything worse than what you haven't already said about yourself; it is an occupational hazard of being you.

"Whoever you are, leave me alone," I say and you are mouthing the same words. How do I know what is going through your mind? And, more importantly, why would an overgrown frat boy care to poke his finger in your dank and moldy psyche?

As if I have a choice.

We stand facing each other. You are blocking my way but are afraid to slink away, trying to ignore my laughter and my awful monologue about inadequacy that is the de facto soundtrack of your life; a spoken word performance that only gets worse with your eyes closed.

I can't take it and have to shut you up. "You like the way that sounds. 'The soundtrack of your life.' It sounds deep, doesn't it? It could almost masquerade for wit if it weren't stupid. Oh, I'm sorry. Did I hurt your feelings? I forgot how sensitive you are about your intelligence. Do you really think life is fair? If you aren't an athlete, then you are compensated with a superior intellect? Sorry, it doesn't work that way. You have no athletic skills and are also a dolt."

"Who are you?" you ask, trying to calm your quivering voice. You feel like an antelope fully in the jaws of a lion, glassy-eyes, complicit in your demise.

"Oh, that's a nice one, too. Too bad it's nonsense, too. Antelopes aren't complicit in their own deaths. They just die."

You're panicking and start running down the street. Unburdened by the need to be secretive, I easily keep pace with you. "You're pathetic. This is the best you could come up with, indignantly running away? One question, to where? Where do you have to go?" Your footsteps are easy to follow in the slush, which will readily melt with the slightest rise in temperature, erasing all trace of you. You are trying to ignore the chorus of my voice in unison with the words parading through your mind.

You turn and look at me, seeking pity. "Are you my conscience or something?"

"Being your conscience," I sniff, "would imply that I give a damn about you. And, besides, do you think I would want be the conscience for a loser like you? Me?" You actually look guilty.

"Pathetic," I say, crossing my arms. We both know what I mean.

"But you know exactly what was going on in my mind. Are you a dream?"

"Do I seem like a dream?"

"More like a nightmare."

I've been called worse. "No, I'm real. Are you going to get to the point soon? Do you really think if you talk long enough you'll come up with something intelligent? It doesn't work for the monkeys with the typewriters, and it doesn't work for you. Okay, since I am busy and you're stuck, let me try to explain it to you. I'll use small words. And stop fantasizing about telling me to fuck off. You don't have the *cojones*. The best way I can explain it to you is, I am that voice in your head."

"You're the voice in my head? All the voices?"

"How many voices are there?"

"Well, I guess two. There's one that just seems like mine. And then there is one who tells me how bad I . . . " you trail off when you see me smiling.

"That's me."

"You're the voice of doubt in my head?"

"Voice of doubt. Voice of truth. Pick it. That's me." You stare at me with disbelief. "No charge," I smile. "Oh, shit, you're not going to ask more questions, are you? Look if you are looking for this to make sense, it won't. At least not to you. Can't we just leave it at that?"

"Why?" is all you can mutter.

"I knew you were going to ask me that question. You're not going to accept 'why not,' are you? Look, I said it's complicated. Just accept I'm here for a reason."

"You are? Making me doubt myself—basically everything I do. How is that positive?"

"Who said anything about it being positive? I call it like I see it. And," I pause, squinting, "I can't say I am impressed."

A bucket of nausea drops in your stomach as you try to prioritize your questions. What was the point of delaying the inevitable? You won't understand, so why explain? The next question will be, "Who are you?"

I hate that question. "What does it matter who or even what I am? I'm the guy who expresses his opinion. You don't go around asking bloggers why they believe what they do, do you?"

"But everything you say is negative."

"Call 'em like I see 'em."

"But you can't be right all the time. I . . . I can't be wrong all the time, can I?"

I sigh. "Look, I didn't say I am right. All I said is I express my opinion. It's not my fault you take everything I say as gospel. You disagree with me, or ignore me. No skin off my nose. I get paid whether you listen or not. Are we done? I really shouldn't be talking with you. Strictly against policy."

"You talk with me every minute of every day."

"No. No. I talk to you every minute of every day. I'm not supposed to talk with you. I have already said too much. Trust me, nothing good can come of this. Nothing." Now it is my turn to walk away, hoping you won't follow me.

"Wait, you said you were paid to talk with me. Paid by whom?"

"None of your business."

"It's none of my business who is paying you to whisper crap

in my ear every day?"

"Nope. He wants it that way."

"He? It's a man?"

"Aw, Christ, this is why you are such a loser. You ask dumb questions. I needed a pronoun. I used "he." If I said "she" you would have gone all moist and accuse me of working for your mother. Can I use 'it' if it will shut you the hell up? No? Well too Goddamn bad and before you think I am some messenger of the Lord, I ain't. Goddamn it, it is just a fucking expression, got it?"

You look like you just finished a marathon you had run under protest. "How long have you been doing this?"

"How old are you?"

"Forty-four."

"Then I have been doing this for 44 years, 236 days, 12 hours, 23 minutes, and 6, 7, 8 seconds."

"Really, since I was born?" Obviously things have slowly started to make sense to Mr. Shit-for-brains.

"We pride ourselves on our thoroughness."

"What do you mean 'we'? Do you mean there are more of you?"

"Yes, every person has an attendant like me. You're not privileged to be so fucked up. Usually we have something positive to counterbalance the bad stuff." You look depressed. "Sorry to ruin your day. Actually no, I'm not. It's my job."

You tilt your head like you're taking on water. "So all those times when I thought I heard voices in my head, it was you?"

"Yep. Well, I get two weeks' vacation and Sundays off so sometimes it's Steve working with you. But don't worry, he's up on all your failures and sticks pretty much to script."

"So when I was learning to play the drums and couldn't find the beat that was you in my head telling me that I had no rhythm?"

"Actually you have no rhythm. I was just pointing it out. Wait a minute, don't you dare! Don't you fucking dare pin this on me."

"Pin what on you?"

"Pin your failures on me. The fact that you don't have a career. The fact you suck at math. The fact you spend most nights masturbating yourself to sleep. I have nothing to do with that. What could you be if I wasn't destroying your confidence? That's what you are thinking, isn't it?

"I'm just the reporter. The reason you don't have a career is you have no marketable skills. The fact you suck at math is because you suck at math. And the fact you masturbate yourself to sleep at night is because most women recognize a loser when they see one. Oh, and if you think you can pin all this on your mother, don't bother. She sucks, too. You would still suck if June Cleaver were your mother."

"You son of a bitch," you say, spitting out words like seeds. "What did I ever do to you? Do you know what it is like to have nothing but doubts? I am not talking about the big doubts. I mean about everything. What to eat? Whether people like me? What's my life's purpose? What could you possibly gain from this? What's the use of it all? Goddamn it! Why don't you leave me alone?" Your fingers are curled into a fist, but they might as well be a balled-up tissue. We both know you can't intimidate me.

"I can't leave you alone. It's my job." Something odd is going on in my stomach, like I swallowed a brick. Either I am feeling guilt or I have to take an enormous dump. It is an unpleasant and unusual feeling.

You probably think this is some monumental moment. Sadly, I know better. The only answer to, "When will it ever get better?" is "Never."

"This is your job?" you say. "Hell, I would rather be a trash man than do what you do. Up to my nostrils in filth and shit."

This isn't going to end well. But when you fall, you fall hard and I will have plenty of material. I'll be able to phone it in for the next week or so. Go, moron, go.

You, on the other hand, never learn. "When trash men get

home, they're done. And no matter what type of day it's been, it's over. You, you're never done. You'll never be done with me."

You're right, but I'll be damned if I give you the satisfaction. My stomach feels carbonated and I am about to explode. "You couldn't be a trash man; you never throw anything out. You take all that crap in your life and line it up pretty on your shelf like some sort of collection of the pathetic. If you can't be the best, you have to be the worst."

"You don't get it, do you? You don't know what its like to have no place where you feel like you belong, because some asshole is whispering in your ear that your friends are getting tired of hearing you whine. That your family is embarrassed to be around you. That where ever you are, you don't belong."

"Nice try," I say, sighing. "But you are not going to get anywhere. I get it; you're pissed off at me. You keep trying to get away from me. You'll try anything—whiskey, pot, bike riding, household chores, tutoring underprivileged children. All in the hope that you'll push the right button and, poof, I'll go away. But I don't, do I? Can't ask for more dedication than you get from me."

"Thanks a lot," you say with as much sarcasm as you can muster. It's lost on me.

"You're welcome. How do you think I feel? Most of the times when we get someone as screwed up as you, one of three things happen." I make an "L" with my index finger and thumb, put in my mouth and pretend a large caliber bullet is whizzing through my brain. I roll up my sleeve and pantomime injecting myself and letting my jaw drop open and eyelids droop.

"What's the third thing?" you ask.

"They grow up. Most people give up on thinking they're someone they aren't by the time they are in their mid-twenties. They get married, have kids, and buy larger TVs. And when they get sad, they have another beer or maybe an affair. But not you. You continue along, miserable, but all too practical to blow your brains out. You keep waiting to be better. And, somewhere in that pea brain of yours, you keep thinking that tomorrow will be better. Who cares if none of the yesterdays were? Tomorrow is always another day. God, your optimism makes me sick. I should have been out of you years ago."

"Why don't you leave then?"

"Don't you get it? I can't. Every morning, I wake up and think this is the day when you finally give up and do it already. But, no, as soon as your eyes open, the whining starts and off to work I go. You think it is easy to tell someone day after day that they suck? Thinking that one day you will listen to me and something will change. But it doesn't. You mope, sulk, and whine and repeat the whole goddamn thing the next day."

"Jesus, you should hear the way they joke about me back at the office. They ask me how my day went when they know damn well it is always the same. Nothing good. Nothing ever will be. Lather. Rinse. Repeat. Why can't you face that you will accomplish nothing? Nothing, except making me miserable. Sometimes I think I am the one who is trapped."

You are about to say something. Something clever, I suppose, but I can't hear it because you are laughing. "Why are you laughing? Stop it. I know what you are thinking. You can't expect me to keep showing up day after day. It isn't fair. Stop laughing at me. Stop it."

Veal

(for Mark)

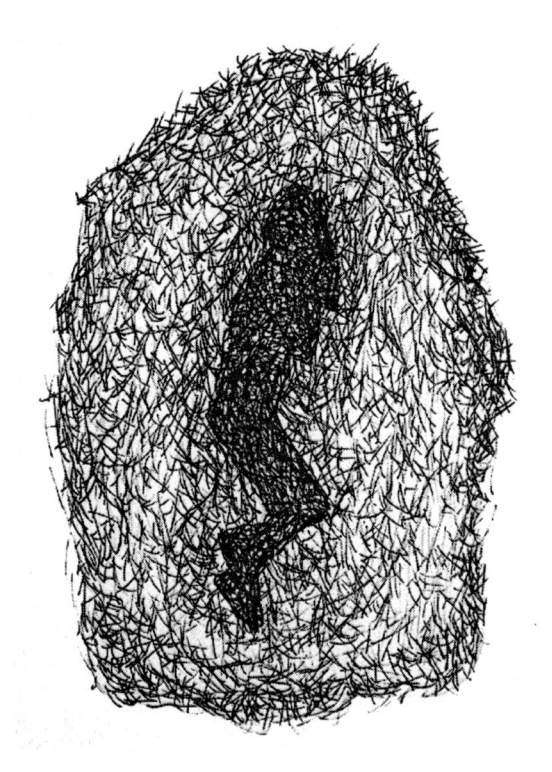

She took the jar of milk from my hand. "You want any more?

"Huh?" I asked, without taking my eyes from my TV; Bobby Flay was feeding chuck into a grinder.

"You're not listening to me. You know I hate it when you don't listen to me. So do you want some more milk?" She sighed impatiently at any delay of the inevitable.

"I would rather have a burger."

"You know the doctor says meat would be bad for you."

"What doctor? I haven't been out of this pen in years and nobody but you and occasionally Dad come by to see me. And when he does, he barely says anything."

"Your father is not much of a talker. Consider yourself lucky." She screwed the lid back on the jar. Her hand seemed embarrassed, unable to look me in the eyes.

"I don't feel lucky," I muttered into one of my chins, hoping she couldn't hear me. She hated when I contradicted her, and bad things happened when I did.

"Let's not start this again," she said like a black sky to the west. "I got you a television didn't I? It's not my fault you watch cooking shows all day. I don't know why you torture yourself. You get over a hundred channels on that thing. Find something else besides the Food Network to watch."

I liked watching celebrity chefs cook dishes I would never make or taste. "Let me out and I will find another topic to discuss. We can even talk about you for a change."

She stuck her face in the window. It wasn't her whole face as the opening was too small. All I could see were her nostrils down to the top of her chin. Her lips were full and some of the deep, red lipstick she wore late into her sixties stained her incisors. All the wrinkles pointed south.

"You keep saying you want to get out. Believe me; you wouldn't like it out here. It's a terrible place—full of cruel, selfish people who would hurt you as soon as say good morning." She turned around as if someone were about to plunge a knife into her back. She was disappointed no one was there. "One day you will thank me for your nice warm pen. Do you want any more milk or not?"

"Not," I said and turned over to get comfortable on the bedding that I had piled up as a pillow under my head. It was better than the hay that lined the floor of the pen until five years ago when my mother found a "premium" bedding that was made from the byproducts of pulp mills and was fifty percent more absorbent than traditional bedding.

She accused me of being ungrateful for the upgrade. Not only did it cost more, but it required a trip to the other side of town to a pet superstore. For years, our neighbor Mr. Ruhnquist simply delivered hay directly to our farm, leaving it outside of the barn for my mother to fork in before it rained. Mr. Ruhnquist was not a curious man and never asked why my mother needed so little hay or why he never heard any animals in the barn.

"Nobody appreciates what a mother does for her child, least of all her child." I had to admit that the bedding was more than fifty percent more comfortable than hay, but if I had my druthers I would prefer to sleep in a bed.

My mother fed me a concoction that she called milk, but was fortified with all the nutrients I needed to be healthy. Because I could not fully stand up in my pen and could only crawl along its seven-foot length, she made sure to keep the calories on the light side.

Even though I never tasted it, I craved meat. A knife slicing through flesh fascinated me. I imagined holding a knife and carving into flesh. I pinched my ample stomach and wondered what it would be like to have someone slice into me. Would it hurt? Based on what I saw on television, I couldn't imagine it would. The beef seemed so willing.

Have you ever watched someone who loves meat eat it? They cut a small piece and pause with the tines of the fork just inches away from their mouth and then, as if they can't stand the temptation any longer, slide it in and chew. Chew, with eyes closed, noiselessly. I had teeth and I had a tongue, but I just didn't have the mechanics. I would open and close my mouth but, if I had a mirror, I assumed I would look like I was having some sort of seizure. If you look closely at a meat lover there's a little shiver of pleasure that slips down his spine as he chews. All I knew from shivering was winter when the wind would make the plastic walls feel like ice.

My mother was wearing her disappointment pout. I knew what was coming; the story of her life. There was no point in recounting my biography: Born. Lives in a pen.

My mother's story was rich with perpetual disappointment. She was born Wilma Ellsworth Hutchinson and appended Eckhoff to it when she defiantly married my father, the silent farmer. She was the only child of Dr. Ward Hutchinson III, a successful surgeon and the author of *Spine Trauma and Intervention*, first and second editions.

"Even your grandmother, my mother, referred to him as Dr. Hutchinson the third," my mother explained to me for over the fifty-ninth time. I wished, for the fifty-ninth time, that I had not thought of making a hash mark on the wall of my pen earlier so I could hold it over my mother.

My mother spoke in a dreamy voice. "Imagine Dr. Hutchinson the third's disappointment when he learned that there would be not a fourth. Not only was I not the son he had been expecting, but, due to complications of my birth, there was little hope that my mother would ever be able to have another child."

"He held me at arm's length as if someone would be there presently to replace me with his rightful son. When no one came, he handed me back to my mother and announced he required some time alone and would return in a few days to bring us home. And with that, he was gone, walking away with his long fingers intertwined behind his back."

"Your grandmother, my mother," my mother said, unbidden, completely obscuring the finer points of making pork tinga, "told me that he never held me unless it was an emergency and then would resent the interruption." Through my hole, all I could see were her teeth, one with a gold cap. Though her voice was sad, her teeth betrayed no emotion. They were for chewing and nothing else. And judging by the several editions of chin that came into view occasionally, it was something she did quite often. I was dying to know what they chewed last.

She continued in chorus to the voices in her head: "To my father, love was an invention of perverted psychiatrists who were desperately seeking relevance and explanation for their own sense of inadequacy. He thought they were missing the point. The reason they feel inadequate was that they were inadequate. Otherwise they would have pursued a genuine medical profession. He thought psychiatry was a scam. If he was not too busy practicing actual medicine, he would have written an article on it.

"According to him, children do not need to feel their father's love; they need to feel their father's expectations. If they do not live up to his expectations, they require his disapproval as a method for improvement. It was the only way we may progress as a species. If we coddle children, we have failed in our duty to our civilization. And then what would we have? A society of psychiatrists.

"Whenever my mother, your grandmother, held me out to him, he would stare at me as if I was infectious. 'Children have mothers for the softer arts.' And by softer arts, he meant anything that could not be dissected and slipped under the microscope.

"It was very simple. He would not recognize me as a person until I had deserved recognition. And I had already had disappointed him by not being a male. If I were to be recognized, I would have to claw my way out of the hole. Until that time he would provide me with shelter, food, and clothing as was his obligation. What my mother decided to do was her business, so long as it did not require anything beyond the above-mentioned list of duties or the use of psychiatrists." She sighed and waited for sympathy.

Today I had had enough. Bobby was now grilling rib-eyes with a chipotle-pineapple glaze. What was the point of this story, any way? Would it end any differently? Would listening mean she would let me out of my pen? No, if anything it only confirmed her decision to keep me "safe."

"Mother, I've heard this story. All of it. If you want me to understand why you locked me in a pen for all of my life, don't bother, I get it. You want to keep me safe. There's no need for metaphor. If you want me to forgive you, forget it. I'm not going to do it. Besides, Bobby's grilling steaks. And I want to hear." I turned on my side and reached over for the remote to turn the TV up as loud as possible.

My mother walked to the other side of the pen and put her mouth by the small ventilation hole, the one next to the TV. "You're just as bad as he was. Only interested in yourself. Maybe this isn't about you. Have you considered that? No, it is like the world begins and ends with you."

Of course the world started and ended with me, or, to be more precise, started and ended with the plastic walls of my pen. For all I knew, other than my interaction with my mother, the 100-plus channels on my satellite TV and the sounds of my father's boots going by were all that existed.

My mother's lips were determined. I had two choices, either give in and listen to her story or finally utter those words she had been waiting to hear for as long as I could remember. She even offered several times to let me out to stretch my legs if only I would tell her I knew she was only looking out for my best interests. But I would be damned if I even came close to "you were right." To the very core of my pliable bones, I was resolute she would never hear me utter those words.

Bobby had moved on, to ribs. Ribs make me drool; what does it feel like to rip flesh from the bone with your teeth? I slip my stubby fingers across my chest, trying to feel the bone beneath the fat. What was in the mop he was brushing on them—vinegar, tomato sauce, Worcestershire sauce, molasses, and what else? What was the secret ingredient? Jesus, I can't hear anything with her yapping on about my ingratitude. My ingratitude? I would be grateful if she shut the hell up for once!

"He was right. I don't mean about you. I mean about his role. He earned the money, but wasn't affectionate. Grandmother got to stay home and had plenty of love. You got love from someone at least. What do I have? A mother who locked me in a pen and a father who doesn't talk."

"You think it's that easy?"

"From here, everything looks easy. The hardest thing I have to do every day is gather my soiled bedding in a bucket. So far as I can tell, life is pretty much a breeze."

"Your life is a breeze because I make it a breeze. I attend to your every need so you don't have to. Try being out here. You would see that it isn't so easy."

"Deal," I said, but she wasn't listening. The only voice she heard was her own.

"You really take love for granted, don't you? You always assume that someone will love you because they're supposed to love you. I know I have created an unreal world in that little box of yours. I know you don't understand why I did it. But you are just going to have to take it on faith I did it because I love you. I can tell you the alternative is a lot worse. Without a parent's protection you feel totally vulnerable. At any moment, something awful might happen and probably will. You will never understand the cold, hard look of a father's disapproval."

She might have been right. I wasn't sure what my father thought of me as he rarely came into the barn. For nearly twenty-five years, I thought he was dead or at least gone. It was only when I kept hearing someone walking outside the barn door in rubber boots that I demanded to know the truth about my father. I refused to drink my milk for two days before she agreed to ask him to visit me. But, she warned me, he wasn't much of a talker so I shouldn't be disappointed.

Once a week or so, I would hear the familiar scraping of his boots on the concrete floor. He would stand maybe 10 feet away from me so all I could see was the bottom of his overall tucked into his muddy boots.

I had never heard my father actually speak. Most of the time, he would cough and wheeze and leave it to me to interpret. "Cough. Wheeze. You. Cough. Wheeze. Okay? Cough." To which I would say, "I'm okay, Dad." There was no point in asking about getting out of the pen, because he would say: "Cough. Wheeze. Ask. Cough. Wheeze. Mother. Cough."

Maybe that is why my mother married him. After all the awful things my grandfather had said to her, it must have been a relief to be with someone who never spoke. She told me he was simple farmer who stood six feet tall, but weighed less than 130 pounds when she met him at a farmer's market. He had parked his dented, red pickup truck on the far end of the parking lot. He lowered the tailgate and offered a selection of cauliflower, broccoli, and cabbage. He had torn off the top of a cardboard box and scrawled "Eckhoff Farms" in marker. "He ran out of room and the M and the S ran up the side of the sign. Your father," "was never good with words."

My mother was smitten by what she took to be his quiet confidence and his inability to express himself in anything that did not involve seed and manure. "Imagine my shock when I learned the only reason he was quiet was that he had nothing to say. He was not much of a listener either. That took me years to figure out, too. I thought his nodding signified understanding. He just needed something to do with his head."

"He didn't even stand up for me the one time he met my father to announce our engagement. My father called down all the fury of heaven on us and our eventual imbecile progeny. And all your father did was sit there and cough into his hand and nod. The only good your father did in this world was to be the cause of the fatal heart attack that took your grandfather two months before you were born."

"Cough. Wheeze. Need. Cough. Wheeze. Anything? Cough," he asked, sounding like he was trying to swallow his fist.

He might as well have asked me if I wanted to sprout wings. According to my mother, he was not a problem solver. He was a farmer and was comforted by routine. Spring was to be wet; summer, warm; and autumn, cool. And sadly the best he could hope for was no surprises and no changes. "Your father doesn't like change," she would tell me when I asked her what he thought about me being locked up in the pen. "You've been in there so long, I don't know what he would do if he actually met you."

I gave up years ago asking him to unlock the pen. If I even mentioned it, he wouldn't be back for a month. I could hear his shuffling boots outside the barn door. They would pause by the door, and maybe the latch on the door would rattle, but he would walk on. It wasn't worth upsetting him. When you live in a world consisting of two other people, you notice a fifty percent reduction in population.

"Cough. Wheeze. Nice talking. . .cough, wheeze, yawn. . .to. . . cough. Wheeze. Bye."

"Nice talking to you, too, Dad."

The boots receded, accompanied by a sigh that said so much, but accomplished so little.

All these voices (my mother's, my father's, Bobby's) were closing in on me. Every voice but mine. None of this was my fault. I didn't do anything to deserve this life. I wasn't my grandfather and I wasn't my father. What gave her the right to lock me away? I kicked at the door to my pen as I did at least three times a day. But thirty-eight years of being on my back led to severe muscle weakness; the door barely shivered when my foot rapped against it. Goddamn it, even if I could get out of this pen, I would be no better than a blob of jelly on the barn floor.

Fine, I was to spend the rest of my days in this goddamned pen, drinking that chalky shit. All in the name of never knowing someone else's disappointment. But that didn't mean I had to sit here and have her tell me how miserable her life has been for the more-than-the-fifty-ninth time.

My mother was somewhere when she was seven and tried to snuggle against her father when he lay on his bed with a cold cloth on his head as the result of a migraine. "You would think I was some sort of animal, the way he jumped out of bed."

"Mom." Bobby and his incredibly attractive fans were toasting each other with beer, while folding the pork tinga tacos into their mouths.

"All I wanted to do was make him feel better."

"Mom." The blonde with the large breasts looked drunk and was leaning on Bobby's freckled arm, holding it like a tenderloin.

"Just to make him feel better and maybe, just maybe, I could feel capable of making someone feel better."

"Mother!" Bobby looked down at the blonde and smiled at me with a pork shred stuck between his incisors and told me he would be back right after commercial. I had time for this fight now.

"What?" It was almost as if I were waking her from a nap.

"Just shut up. Please shut up. I don't want to hear this again. Not today. Please leave me alone."

"You want me to leave you alone? Is that what you want?" Her voice sounded like a parrot's in the process of being choked. "You don't know what feeling alone is. You think you are all alone in that pen of yours. You don't know alone until you fail to get someone you love to love you back. That's what feeling alone is."

"Stop feeling sorry for yourself. It won't make you feel any better."

She sniffed and I could hear her dabbing her hand across a moist nose. She took a step backward, disappearing from my view. "No, it won't, but I thought of all people you would listen to me. That's all I wanted. But apparently that's too much to ask of my son who I have personally cared for all these years. Why don't you go back to your cooking show and see if they feed you."

I heard the sound of her boots receding and waited for the rusty hinges of barn door to open in complaint. But they didn't and I assumed she was giving me one more chance to apologize. Either that or she was trapped, too.

I turned back to the television set and Bobby was in credits already. He was dancing with the blonde girl who was desperately trying not to drop her margarita as he bumped against her. I hated the show that came after Bobby and flipped off the set. She wants to stew in her silence, I could, too. Eventually my father would be curious about her absence and then we could have it out.

The wind outside howled as if our silence made it uncomfortable. I could hear her quietly crying. I tried not to look, but I eventually put my eye up to the ventilation hole. I could barely see the barn door and only the right leg of my mother. She was wearing dark corduroys and my father's boots. This time I didn't need the cold to make me shiver.

If I pushed her away, what if she stayed away? I not only depended on her for food and a steady supply of fresh bedding, she was now my only connection to the world.

I always felt that I had the upper hand in our relationship because she had wronged me. I held the moral high ground. But realistically, she was the one who held the keys, literally and figuratively. What good did being right do me? If she decided that she had enough, there was nothing to stop her from leaving me alone.

I flipped one of the flaps of my stomach. There was a lot of me and I assumed it would take me quite awhile to consume my vast fat reserves. I would linger in painful hunger and loneliness. I could call out as much as I wanted, but no one would hear me. Or care. To die alone, unnoticed, completely ignored by humanity that wasn't even aware I existed. I lifted myself up and looked at my profile carved into the bedding. This would be the only impression I would make on the earth. "Wait," I called to my mother, "I'm sorry. Don't go."

"I am not going anywhere," she said, walking back to the pen, accompanied by the squelching sounds of my father's boots. She snaked her hand through the window and stroked my jowls. I wrapped my doughy hands around hers. I will never tire of feeling her touch. I imagine this is what a hamburger feels like—warm and juicy.

"Go ahead, Mom. I'll listen. I promise to listen."

"I know you will, Ward. You've always been a good boy."

Straight and Narrow

I instruct my patients to imagine a big balloon floating over their heads with a string attached to their spines. In this manner they will walk with proper posture without seeming mechanical or putting their vertebrae under undue stress.

Other doctors will tell you to imagine the cable is being tightly drawn as if by a divine hand. People who follow this advice tend to fall into two categories: those who wander around like Frankenstein's monster and consequently further damage their cartilage, and those who give up completely and assume that they are not destined for either grace or comfort. They stagger into my office, convinced they have failed and deserve punishment.

But if you imagine a balloon above your head instead of God's hand, your spine and head remain in perfect alignment and you will be able to bend and adjust to life's uneven paths. Besides, I say, with the practiced smile of having repeated this talk for decades now, you will feel more at peace with your pain.

Most of my patients look at me as if I am sort of a New Age lunatic, assuming I know less than the doctors who advised rigidity. They stand up, ostensibly to leave, but I watch their shoulders relax and their heads list like a beach ball on a gentle sea. Their backs, still straight, become elastic as if they were made of rubber instead of steel. You can even see it in their fingers as they relax from a fist to a more natural position. They smile and ask me if this is all they need to do to avoid crippling back pain.

My smile becomes benevolent and sympathetic as I explain there is further treatment required, whether it be surgery, physical therapy or pharmaceuticals. But adjusting their posture and consequently their attitude will take them a great deal down the road to reducing the pain that has haunted their lives like an undisciplined child. "Proper posture is about controlled relaxation and often times distracts the child," I tell them. They thank me, many assuming I have just accomplished a small miracle.

Shirley, my wife of forty years, and Ben, my middle child of thirty-seven, are eager to point out the inherent hypocrisy of my advice. For while I believe controlled relaxation is essential to a healthy spine, I contend it is absolutely the wrong way to conduct one's life.

For as long as I care to remember I have liked order. There is a picture of me as a young teenager, shortly after my father's acquittal, standing on the concrete stairs of our home. My hair is greased and parted to the right. My hands are at my side like a soldier's. I am wearing my gray school suit with a perfectly vertical tie, secured to my neck with an impeccable full Windsor knot. Staring directly into the camera, I am challenging the photographer to find something humorous or endearing about the scene. It would have been a near perfect shot of confidence had I not been wearing matching wool plus-fours and dark socks, revealing my knobby knees.

Shirley takes the picture off of the mantle to show it to dinner guests as a way to mock me. But I am not the least bit insulted. I wear my fastidiousness as a badge of honor as I have worn silk bow ties every day of my adult life, with the exception of Saturdays and vacations, when I have been known to favor ascots.

As a student, it was obvious the path to a life of ease and significance was derived from study and seriousness of purpose. I ask anyone who differs to prove otherwise. What astounded me was my classmates did not understand this. To watch my classmates struggle with the assignments you would think they were developmentally disabled. But the truth was they were lazy and distracted. They would rather play stickball than study.

I have run into childhood friends when visiting my parents' graves in Jeffrey Manor. They are either unemployed mill workers or soon-to-be unemployed mill workers. They look at my Jaguar, at my custom clothing and my contented carriage and they have the gall to ascribe the adjective "lucky" to me. There is nothing lucky about my life nor is there anything mysterious. I did what I was told to do, pure and simple. The roadmap was available for all. Was it my fault I took advantage of what was clearly available?

In medical school, it seemed only natural I would be drawn to the spine. The entire body hangs from the vertebrae. Without the spine we are merely squid-like creatures, barely able to move our eyes about. The spine is one of the most beautiful structures known to man. It resembles a perfect bouquet of gladiola, offering perfect posture and a lifetime of support if only it were treated with respect and care.

Unfortunately for my patients and fortunately for my bank account, most people take their spines for granted. They assume it can take all manner of abuse from the incorrect lifting of heavy objects to improper foot attire. You would not believe the indignation they wear on their faces when they limp into my office as if they had been betrayed by their backs when in fact it was they who betrayed their spines.

Most people want a panacea to cure their pain and a license to do further damage. You would think I was asking them to take the tonsure and commit themselves to lives of abstinence and inactivity. What I prescribe is a reasonable course of exercise, coupled with a fundamental understanding of the physical limitations of bone and cartilage.

To this day I cannot understand why the simple truth is not sufficient motivation. My family and my colleagues are amused and advise me to "lighten up," as if the truth is a diet option.

Ben is a social worker. I tell him he not only has a soft heart, but also a soft head. Recently, he bored me with his study of people's ability to change. If a person, when presented with a simple choice—change or die—will, nine times out of ten, not be able to change. In order to change they require the support of others in a similar position. The whining must be intolerable.

Ben asked me if I am suggesting this person gets what he deserves to which I answer, of course not. But I will not make excuses for other people nor their inability to do what is in their self-interest. If they make bad decisions, so be it. I am under no obligation to hold their hands and draw them away from the precipice to which they are hurtling. All I can wish them is bon voyage.

Ben complains, "I swear you would be better off if you drank booze once in a while. It might help you relax."

I never developed a taste or desire for alcohol. To me it is a refuge from reality and I have no need to retreat in the slightest. I suppose I could use a drink or two a day for medicinal purposes, but the intoxicating affects are neither beneficial nor desirable and can easily be reproduced with a sensible exercise regimen.

I was highly skeptical when Ben showed up for a dinner one Saturday evening with a small glass bottle of what looked like milk. The label had Cyrillic lettering that I knew was neither Russian nor Ukrainian. It started lucidly with a K Y & M and then degraded rapidly to small b attached to an i.

"What is this?" I asked, holding this relic of the Cold War.

"It's Kumis," Ben said brightly. "Mare's milk from Kazakhstan. Brad," a colleague of his from the university whom I considered to be a mush-headed par excellence, "gave it to me to give to you as a present." Brad favored brightly-colored attire of the roughest cloth as if he were some sort of reformed ascetic. Though way into his forties, he dressed like a teenager, wearing his hair long and his beard infested.

It befuddles me why a university professor would think it is appropriate to go about campus like Rasputin on a bad day. Back in my day, not only did the professors wear jackets and ties, so did the students. We had too much respect for knowledge and ourselves. But, judging by Brad's slovenliness, it is clear that civilization is in trouble. On the few times we invited his partner, whom I presume is female, and him over for dinner, his rumpled beard served as a palimpsest of previous meals. I had images of he and his "friend" grooming each other in whatever yurt they inhabited.

"And he wished me to do what with this beverage," I asked, holding it gingerly between my right index finger and thumb, "other than apply a strong disinfectant?"

"Drink it, of course," he said with a smile similar to that a spider flashes, inviting a fly to its web.

"I assume you neglected to mention that this is 'fermented' mare's milk, as if drinking horse milk is not repulsive enough without fermenting it."

"It has so little alcohol in it, it's barely worth mentioning." He tried and failed to appear casual.

"Which is why you didn't mention it all. Why don't you return this to Brad? He and his friend can use it at their next bacchanal. I do not find the central Asian culture to be interesting, nor their customs the least bit hygienic."

"I just thought you might like to try a bit of local culture before you leave for Astana."

"Astana, being?"

"The capital of Kazakhstan," he said cheerfully. "Brad secured a lecture opportunity for you at the prestigious Medical University Astana."

I was unimpressed. "Prestigious as in *sole* medical university? In addition, I was unaware I was under consideration for such an honor nor was I aware that I had the slightest interest in being so honored. I treat, as you know, only humans and I assume Astana U serves all sorts of goats, yaks and whatever furry quadrupeds regularly traverse the vaunted halls of the medical school."

"You should probably get all your snide comments out now as you leave in three weeks. It took a considerable amount of effort for Brad to receive the appropriate permission from the Kazakh authorities. This went up to the Vice Health Minister, himself. They say he is very eager to attend your lecture as well."

"Imagine his disappointment when I am not there."

"I wanted to give this to you as a sixty-fifth birthday present. Think of it as an adventure."

"I am likewise unaware that I was interested in an adventure. And if I was, I doubt Kazakhstan would be in the top ten destinations. Please have Brad express my sincere apologies for this unfortunate misunderstanding."

"Dad, please," he said. Ben only calls me "Dad" when he wants something. He had obviously invested a considerable amount of effort and emotion in this fool's errand. I am not a heartless man, but I had no interest in participating in his delusion.

"Let me discuss this with your mother. This affects her as much as me. I promise I will consider it." I do not relish lying, but sometimes it is prudent to allow the truth to be protractedly revealed. "But, in the interim, please return this bottle to Brad as I do not drink alcohol." I thought Ben walked into the family room because he was hurt; not, as it turned out, to seek reinforcements.

I was surprised by the response of Shirley, who I assumed would be as astonished as I by Ben's temporary insanity, imagining me dressed in some sort of turban or whatever was the anthrax-laden headdress of choice in Astana. Instead, the madness was infectious. Shirley, in a word, was angry. Unfortunately, she was angry with me.

"For once in your life, can you look beyond the borders of your condescending nose?"

I lifted my glasses to my forehead and crossed my eyes as if I was considering what could possibly be wrong with my nose. Finding nothing, I replaced my glasses, placed an innocent smile on my face and shrugged.

Shirley was not amused. Her exasperation sounded like a gas leak before an explosion. I should have known better. Shirley and Ben have always had a kinship that I could not penetrate. The other two children are mine. Owen, our oldest, is the CFO of a hedge fund firm. He is handsome, brilliant and absolutely humorless. Tanya, our youngest, is an attorney in the M & A department in a London law firm. Tanya is not a generous woman. Perhaps that is why she hasn't been home in nearly a year, depriving us the opportunity to see her twin girls, Amelia and Olivia. It is too much hassle, she hisses.

But Ben is all Shirley. He has her eyes and her heart. Both spent their time in the softer side of Yale, Shirley in Linguistics and Ben in Sociology. Of our children, Ben is the one we see the most and, the truth be told, the most fun to have around. Owen and Tanya are purebreds, while Ben revels in his mongrel nature. In rare moments, I envy him his freedom in the same way I admire a gull on an ocean breeze. But as I will never be able to fly, there is no point in wishing for it.

The surest way to annoy Shirley is to hurt Ben's feelings and this time I had excelled in fanning the flames of her ire. "You truly are incapable of considering anyone's feelings because of the device you call a heart. Can't you see Ben wants to do this for you? That he thinks that perhaps this will do you good?"

"You make me sound as if I need pity. I honestly did not ask for anyone's sympathy nor am I comfortable accepting it." I might as well have been debating a brick wall. Ben had been hurt and retribution must be exacted.

"Can't you think of it as a change in scenery?" She was so upset that she had difficulty making eye contact.

"I have no problem with the present scenery." I said, walking into the kitchen with the dishes, which is so rare it can't be mistaken as anything but a signal of my annoyance and the end of the discussion. But Shirley would have none of it and followed me. I do not like to lose my temper, but I am not afraid to do so. "Would it make you feel better if I get dysentery and am sodomized by some migratory animal?"

"Please don't add repulsiveness to insensitivity. You are going to Kazakhstan. Look, we can argue about this for the next three weeks. But you are getting on that plane and you are going to give those lectures. You have the vacation time and you owe us a little flexibility after all these years of us putting up with your intransigence."

Looking up from the glass I had been rinsing continuously, I said: "I was not aware that you were keeping an account. Had I known I would have not allowed myself to fall so in debt."

Shirley was undeterred. We both knew I had lost. She would continue to badger me until I surrendered, if only for the peace's sake. "You are entitled to be miserable and I will allow you to make snide comments, but I won't allow you to disappoint our son. He's very proud of you and for once you can earn it. You are going, so please let's stop arguing. Why don't you move on to another glass? That one's clean."

I shrugged. I am not a fan of admitting defeat and preferred it to be inferred from my lack of engagement. Besides I had placed my faith in post-Soviet bureaucratic incompetency. I imagined us at the Air Astana counter as a woman of heft in an orange polyester jump suit with matching neck scarf explain to us that our papers were not in order and she could not allow us to board the rusting 707 bound for Kazakhstan. I would shrug at Shirley and motion that my hands were tied. I would even feign disappointment, but we both knew I would be dancing a jig if appropriate.

Unfortunately for me, old habits die easily when foreign currency is involved. The Kazakh Health Ministry had arranged for all necessary visas and had booked us on United Airlines from Chicago to London in first class. Everyone involved seemed excited by my pilgrimage and I wondered if the entire country suffered from sciatica and found yak milk enemas to be ineffective.

The Vice Minister had arranged for us to stay overnight at the Savoy before catching a flight to Astana. The champagne and caviar that awaited us were perfectly chilled and served impeccably. While I did not partake in the champagne, it did my heart good to see Shirley shiver with delight as the bubbles disappeared down her throat. She asked me if I wanted any and I quickly shook my head and, for once, she was not disappointed to drink alone.

While not exceptionally luxurious, our flight to Astana (via Almaty) was gracious and remarkably efficient. It seemed everyone we encountered knew of my skepticism and did everything in their power to disappoint me by anticipating all my needs. The flight to Astana was remarkably uneventful. We were seated in the front row of a 767 and attended by a young man who spoke earnest, if imperfect, English. He had the wide slanted eyes suggesting it was not long since his ancestors galloped across the frozen steppes under fur-lined caps. He called me "Sir Doctor" whenever our eyes met.

The food was unremarkable, but was the appropriate temperature and plentiful. My wife gingerly tasted the Russian sparkling wine, which the steward insisted on calling "Frenches Shampainey" and declared it not bad and handed the flute to me. Reclined and relaxed in the slippers they had provided, I almost brought the glass up to my lips. But I caught myself and narrowed my eyes at Shirley who shrugged.

On arriving in Astana, we were met by a pretty woman, dressed all in white, including knee-high leather boots. She wore a leather newsboy cap, tilted jauntily over one of her dark eyes. She didn't speak English, but simply smiled broadly and giggled whenever we asked her a question.

The Hotel Astana was located in the center of the city and was surprisingly contemporary. The hotel staff had ramrod perfect posture, holding their hands out to firmly shake ours for the slightest excuse. I must have shaken hands with the bell boy six times from the time we met at registration to when he showed me how the mirrored door slid open to reveal a closet hidden behind.

The room was perfectly satisfactory, well-apportioned and could have been located in any European city. The view from the 18th floor showcased the contemporary architecture that seemed built to be especially appreciated from the Nursultan suite of the Hotel Astana. There was a bottle of genuine French champagne and a tin of Russian sevruga, the size of my fist.

The whole atmosphere of our Astana visit was one of obsequious pandering. I wondered if I was the butt of the world's greatest practical jokes or they had mistaken me for some resurrected mythological creature. I noticed the waiter at breakfast reverently regard my soiled knife before surreptitiously slipping it into the pocket of his starched white jacket. The door man who signaled our limousine stared at the 200 Tenge bill I slipped into his hand. He held the bill so gingerly for fear of crushing it that I was forced to close his fingers so it did not blow away. There were tears in his eyes as we pulled away from the curb.

"All I ask is that you don't let this go to your head; you barely fit through doors now," Shirley said as we drove through the bustling streets, segregated by the tinted windows of the limousine. She was to drop me off at the medical university and then be treated to a tour of the highlights of Astana, personally conducted by the wife of some official. As we approached the medical university, she grabbed my arm and stared at me with a combination of concern and contempt. "Be nice," she grumbled.

A short, young man in a black business suit greeted us as we pulled up to the front entrance to the Medical Academy Astana.

He was dragged several feet as he grasped the handle to the door before the limo came to a complete stop. His only concern was whether I was concerned. "Please do not worry about me. I am very sorry if my clumsiness has caused you distress." He bowed several times and smiled so broadly that I was afraid the tendons in his face would rupture.

He introduced himself as Elemes, Deputy to the Vice Minister of Health. I placed his age around mid-thirties, same age as Ben. He was to be my translator and liaison. I was not to allow any wish to be unfulfilled. He apologized for not meeting us at the airport but he was detained at the medical academy ensuring my day would proceed with absolutely no impediments. He looked at me with the hopeful eyes of a son who feared disappointing his father.

Hanging from the balcony of the two-story domed entrance hall was a banner welcoming their "estimated guest." A few students stood above me and sung a song of welcome that probably sounded better in Kazakh than it did to my Western ears, which equated it to sheep gargling.

A squat man with the square rimmed glasses and the requisite blue-grey suit came up to me with both hands extended as if we were long-lost siblings. He spoke quickly and Elemes, who had been trailing me, only caught the second half of the speech.

Elemes explained that this gentlemen, who refused to let go of my hands, was the honorable Nurzhan Skeker, Vice Minister of Health. It was his great pleasure to welcome me to Kazakhstan in general and the Medical Academy Astana in particular. He was honored to welcome such an accomplished physician and, as a surgeon himself, he looked forward to listening to my lecture and would consider it a great honor if I would allow him to observe an operation.

I paused and looked at Elemes who was smiling like a labrador retriever. As my silence extended, the smile on his face froze and then melted. The Vice Minister was still holding my hands, waiting for my reply. I dared not withdraw his enthusiastic shake. I pasted a smile on my face and whispered to Elemes that there must be some sort of mistake; I was not a surgeon.

He smiled broadly. "You are not doctor?" he asked as if were sharing a joke.

"No, I am a doctor, just not a surgeon. I help people with back pain, but I don't operate on them."

Elemes nodded dolefully. "This is most embarrassing. What should I tell the minister? He will be most disappointed."

"Please tell him I no longer operate. Due to my own back pain, I can no longer stand for long periods of time." I wondered if Kazakhstan had developed irony. I withdrew my hands from the minister's and massaged my lower back, looking sadly at him as Elemes translated.

The smile disappeared from the minister's face. He spoke slowly and with obvious compassion.

"The minister says he sorry he will not be able to see you operate. He suggests you consult a doctor for your pain." I nodded as if I had not considered this idea. The minister placed his arm around my shoulders, which must have been extremely uncomfortable for him as I was at least six inches taller and I could feel nearly his full weight on my shoulders. He steered me to a long table covered with various bottles and trays of food. With his free hand he gestured at the bounty.

Beside the table, wearing a dress of dark blue with gold embroidery and a matching miter with a bright yellow plume, was the oldest woman I had ever seen. Her face looked like the surface of the moon with deep craters and crevices, not the least being her mouth that could not have contained more than thirteen teeth in various stages of decay. She looked more like a piece of furniture than anything else. She obviously was suffering from Kyphoscoliosis, which was so bad she looked like a question mark that had been twisted into two directions. I thought she was brought to me as a patient, until I noticed the tray in her hands.

The raisins were easy enough to recognize, as were what looked to be small round doughnuts. There were other decidedly dairy products that looked like cheese that had been left over from a post-apocalypse party. She also held several empty glasses of dubious cleanliness. Her head listed to the right pointing to the table on which there were several bottles, one being the kymus that Ben tried to poison me with. I resolved to steer clear of it. A few other bottles had different labels and I ignored those as well.

Vice Minister Skeker took me by the elbow and led me to the beverages. He pointed towards the bottles obviously inviting me to choose my poison. I smiled and pointed towards the samovar which he interpreted to be an enormously humorous joke worthy of sputum launching and slaps on the back. He gestured towards the bottles again and the smile froze on his face as if in warning that it would disappear at the next instance of insubordination. My father would get the same look when we argued longer than he thought fit.

"All of these," I asked Elemes, "have alcohol in them?"

"Of course," Elemes said brightly and dutifully. This is kymus that is from horses. This is shubat is from camels and this one is airan from cows. All very tasty and potent."

And all equally repulsive. The choice was unpleasant but not impossible as I would not consider drinking anything that came from a horse or a camel. I pointed to the airan and indicated with index finger and thumb, barely separated, that I would have a small drink.

Judging from my wet face and sore back, Vice Minister Skeker found this hysterical as well. He spoke in gruff tones to the woman who could barely reach the bottle on the table. She took careful aim at my glass and slowly filled it with repulsive slurps of the thick liquid. The Vice Minister spoke to her sharply and she surrendered the bottle without complaint. He grabbed the glass out of my hand and filled it up until only the surface tension and steady hand kept it in place.

Vice Minister Skeker toasted to my health, the health of generations past and present, the general glory of President Nazarbayev and of the Kazakhi people. There were also some references to strong loins and fast horses, but I may be remembering it wrong. For my part, his toast could have been as long as the contents of the Trenton phone book. I would have welcomed anything to come between me and this quivering gelatinous beverage that has been thrust into my hand.

But the toasts came to an end. He held his glass up in expectation that I would hold mine up as well. And then he shoved his glass into mine as if he were trying to merge them. The airan sloshed out of the glass, drenching my hand, cuff and right lapel of my jacket. Vice Minister Skeker did not notice as he was busily emptying the contents of his glass down his throat.

I lifted my glass to my lips. Being no stranger to acrid odor of isopropyl alcohol, I could tell the alcohol content of airan was considerable. I slid the edge of the glass under my lip and took the barest of sips. It burned and then numbed my lips, tongue and throat in that order.

Vice Minister Skeker did not feign amusement by my delicate tasting of the beverage, which compared unfavorably to antifreeze. He took the bottom of my glass and tipped it straight up. Most of the liquid ran down the front of my jacket, but a sufficient amount made it down my throat to cause me to gag and become dizzy simultaneously.

It wasn't unpleasant. It reminded me of waking up and not being able to locate my glasses. Everything seemed to be unfocused and unfamiliar. My stomach was unsettled and none of the fried pies that the crooked woman pushed in front of me appealed to me in the slightest. She smiled with her loathsome teeth. I held my middle and looked unsettled, hoping she would have pity on me. She misconstrued my meaning, believing I would prefer to drink rather than eat. She retrieved a different bottle from the end of the table and handed it to Vice Minister Skeker.

It was the color and consistency of liquid paper and poured malevolently into two soap-stained glasses the woman handed him with her unclean hands. Vice Minister Skeker held the bottle in one and the glasses in the other, secured by his fingers soaking in the liquor. The smile slipped too easily on to his face, indicating the alcohol had begun to depress his central nervous system, weakening his facial muscles. My father once had that look on his face when my mother asked him if he had had one too many gin and tonics before being called to the hospital to perform an emergency appendectomy. He smiled and put on his coat without reassuring her.

The suit that followed the death of the patient was the result of post-operative bleeding stemming from an incompetently tied suture. The trial was mercifully quick and my father's attorney was adept at pointing out the poor health of the patient prior to the operation.

My father was perplexed by the verdict. At dinner, he would hold a wine glass in his hand and stare at his reflection. For a while he swore off alcohol. While the jury found him innocent, he could not help but feel guilty. No matter how many reasons my mother listed why it was not his fault, he would shake his head and explain it was hubris tainted by gin that prompted him to take scalpel in hand that day.

His guilt lasted all of ten days when he casually opened a bottle of burgundy, poured it into the bowl of the glass and quickly drained it. He exhaled loudly through his nostrils and stared out into the night through the dining room window. He seemed as if he was waiting for something malevolent that never came. He filled the glass again and emptied it. Only then did his shoulders relax and a smile escape from his face.

From that night on he would have a drink as soon as he got home and push the unpleasant memory further away. He would toast his victory over guilt and scare it off with a large collection of alcoholic beverages. When he eventually stopped operating (at the suggestion of the general counsel with sharp olfactory sense) and took a teaching position at a state university, it only took three or four drinks before he convinced himself this was his choice.

As a boy, I was crushed by his alcoholism, a point not lost on him. On the nights when he had more rather than less, he would stare at me. "Why do you look at me that way, boy? I have forgiven myself, don't you think it's time you do the same? You should loosen up." He would always have at least one more drink before falling asleep in the arm chair by the fireplace with a contented expression.

It was the same look on the Vice Minister's face as he dangled the glasses in front of my face. I looked at his pudgy fingers in the liquor, wondering where he stood on hygiene outside of the operation theater. My head weighed half of what it did fifteen minutes previous, floating off my shoulders. I had no desire for whatever he was proposing for me to drink, but I also had no desire to refuse it; I was completely ambivalent and for once without an opinion. A wondrous feeling of apathy came over me.

I took the glass with the least amount of finger in it and lifted it to my lips. Closing my eyes, I toasted the health of the minister. I felt his hand on my neck, which had curved slightly forward. When his fingers reached C7, he pushed me forward until my lips kissed the edge of the refilled glass.

Ordinarily, I detest being touched by anyone. But there was a freedom being in his strong grasp. I was his prisoner and had no control over my body or my circumstances. I was free to do whatever he wanted.

Vice Minister Skeker made barking sounds that Elemes gleefully translated as "drink, drink, drink!" He was like a child who was allowed to stay up with the grown-ups.

With my head in this position, I was nearly face-to-face with the old woman with the hunched back; her repulsive tongue with its patchwork of thrush, merely inches from mine, coming closer as if she were about to swallow me whole.

Half Off Until Nine

They had outlined their garbage cans in white, blinking lights.

After half a glass, I couldn't recognize the face staring back at me; as there was an ice cube where my nose should have been, I could be forgiven at least for this. Was this my third drink or fourth? Or fifth? I have never been much of a drinker; a margarita or two when we went out for Mexican, or whatever light beer was on sale at the liquor store. But since yesterday, Jameson's was my drink.

The whiskey rippled as the bottle tapped against the glass. I had my head down, trying to ignore where I was—a south suburban Chicago strip club, which was bad enough had it not also been Christmas Eve and my wife and daughters were waiting for me at home. I was sure everyone could see right through me to the shame underneath.

"You want another?" the bartender asked. His face looked like it had been assembled in a hurry, using spare parts. His nose took up nearly a quarter of his face, which was a good thing as it had to support his enormous plastic-framed glasses with little assistance from his floppy ears. His hair was a mess as if he had assisted Tesla in a failed experiment. He was probably Jewish. I heard Jews volunteer at hospitals on Christmas so Christians could be with their families. Did they volunteer at strip clubs, too? I looked around the club that had no more than five other men and a very bored-looking redheaded girl removing her ruffled blouse. Could I be more pathetic? Clearly not and I raised my glass for a refill.

I wasn't used to feeling sad or much else for that matter. Emotions never made much sense to me. Happy wasn't the opposite of sad; it was just another feeling. If things went well, I was happy. If not, I wasn't. It certainly wasn't the stuff of poetry, but it was far from being wrong either. But my wife Maggie thought I was damaged. It was like blaming the patient for the tumor.

Maggie couldn't accuse me of being two-faced; I was this way in college. Never the life of any party, I was kind, attentive and talked little about myself or not at all. I was the answer to her fantasies as I did nothing but listen to her. We sat in the cafeteria and she complained about her current boyfriend who invariably was mean, arrogant or simply ignored her. She asked me if I minded her whining about other men. I didn't. I had nothing to add to the conversation except: "The guy's a jerk; don't date him."

"You can see through problems and leap to the solution," she said, platonically patting my hand. "I am lucky to have a friend like you." She broke up with this boyfriend only to end up with someone worse. And it was back to the cafeteria to be consoled by me, her good friend.

On the night we first slept together, she invited me for a home-cooked dinner at her apartment, not mentioning that her roommate had gone home for the weekend. We sat on her couch watching Saturday Night Live and eating coconut-custard pie with a soggy crust. She thanked me for being there for her. She knew it was a lot (it wasn't) and she had done a lot of thinking about our relationship (I hadn't) and had come to the decision that the problem wasn't with them (her boyfriends) but with her (what was wrong with her?)

Maggie placed her lips close to mine like she was asking me to check for splinters. She closed her eyes and waited. When she opened one eye, I knew she was interested in more than sympathy. It would be silly to refuse the offer and soon my tongue was on hers.

Maggie says it was a special night, although I can't remember much of what happened after we fell into her bed. When she talks this way I have learned to smile and nod. People who knew both of us were surprised we were a couple. We had so little in common, not the least of which was being from different sides of the campus, Maggie in the humanities building where she was a French Literature major and me hunched over a monitor in the Computer Center.

Maggie was all in when it came to relationships. I was never one for card games. I was not much of a programmer, but I could always find other's coding mistakes; I liked finding them as much as I liked being with Maggie. What more was there to talk about?

Maggie suggested we live together during our senior year. I said yes because I could cut my housing expenses by almost a third and sex would be readily available. She saw us as engaged to be engaged while I saw us as what our eldest daughter, Kim, calls "friends with benefits." One of the benefits being I could afford a larger hard drive for my IBM PC XT.

"This is pretty sad, isn't it?" a voice, preceded by a cloud of sweet perfume, said from the next stool. If you removed the layers of makeup, her face could not be much older than Kim's. She was wearing a see-through robe trimmed in fake white fur over her red and silver bra and panties. She had a long face with wide lips painted dark red that made her look carnivorous. She flipped her frizzy brown hair over her shoulder trying to look alluring but settled for bored.

"What's sad?" I asked the rim of my glass.

She spoke in fragments. "This. Us. Tonight. Here."

"You mean being in a strip club on Christmas Eve?"

"Kinda. Except I don't have any other place to be." The bartender looked up as if he had been sleeping. She flashed an insincere wink. "Do you want me to dance for you?" she asked loudly. He nodded and went back to resting his bored chin on his fist.

"Excuse me?"

"Sorry, if I didn't offer Ed would tell Roy, my boss, and there would be hell to pay. Unless you want one. It's half off until nine."

"Half off lap dances on Christmas Eve?"

She shrugged. "It's supposed to get people in the door." She looked around and shrugged again. "Not that it works. I asked Roy why we bother to open on Christmas Eve. He says we are a service business and the public needs to be served. Don't see him here tonight, do you? So do you want one?"

"No," I said quickly, unable to bear the idea of her dancing while yawning at our reflections in the mirror behind the bar.

"Buy me a drink then," she asked, "to celebrate the season?"

"Do you want eggnog?" I said, gesturing for the bartender.

"I'll take a cosmopolitan, Ed," she said. He looked at me; I nodded. Ed went off to retrieve the bottles and the shaker. He popped a cranberry and a plastic piece of holly in her glass. "Merry Christmas," he said.

She leaned forward to sip from the edge of her martini glass the way my daughters drank juice when they were little. "I'm Boo," she said, shaking with an ice-cold hand.

"Boo?"

She shrugged. "Roy gave me that name. He says it's sexy. Works better on Halloween. She picked the plastic leaf out of her glass and stuck it behind her ear. "Maybe I should change my name for Christmas. How's Holly?"

"It'll do."

"And your name? You don't have to tell me if you don't want. I'm not supposed to ask. Most men in here don't want anyone to know their names."

"It's okay. I am Robert. Rob. Most people call me Bob. Nice to meet you Boo or Holly. Merry Christmas." She had the saddest laugh I ever heard. "Did I say something funny?"

"Not really," she said. "It's just spending Christmas here." She leaned forward and wrapped her lips around her pink drink. "Probably the last place I would want to be. Where would you be if you weren't here?"

"Home," I said.

"Home," she said like it was a foreign word. "What home?"

"My home. With my wife and daughters."

"She kick you out? I know what that's like."

"Kick me out? No. She expects me home any moment. She's probably holding dinner for me."

"So why are you here?"

"I don't know. Maybe I want to feel sad; this seems to be a good place to do that."

She nodded and pursed her lips. "It's perfect." She reached out and took the stem of her glass and put it to her mouth, but didn't drink. Her cheap bracelets jingled against the side of the glass. "Why do you want to be sad? Most people are sad when they come in here. They don't come looking for it. If I had my choice, I would never be sad again. But I wouldn't be here if I had a choice."

"You don't have a choice?"

"Not really. It's okay. It used to bother me. Some people get choices and others get choices made for them. I made a lot of bad decisions, so maybe it's best if I don't have a choice anymore."

Ed came back and looked at us suspiciously. Boo squeezed my left thigh. "It's okay, Ed. We're flirting."

"So what did you do?" she asked, leaning an unsure head on her palm. "Why are you here instead of being home with your family?" She smiled into her long fingernails, waiting for me to confess. Who had I slept with? Her best friend? Her sister? Or did she cheat on me with the newspaper boy?

"It wasn't anything like that."

"Is business bad? Some people here are sad because their business is so bad. That's why they don't tip good. They still make me listen to them, though."

"Things are never bad for people in computer consulting. People are always screwing up their systems with viruses and worms and they pay a lot for you to say nothing when they swear they've never been on a porn site."

"People lie to you; that's why you're sad?"

"Not really. It's not my business. I don't judge them and I don't care if they judge me."

"You're lucky," Boo said. "People do nothing but judge me."

"My wife Maggie thinks I judge her when she gets upset. I just don't get worked up about things. We were on our honeymoon in Hawaii. Someone stole her purse. She was out of her mind. To me, it was simply a matter of calling the police and the credit card companies. What's the big deal? You would think I stood by while she was raped."

"She felt violated. It can be worse, believe me. I used to work for this guy who makes Roy look like a saint. He used to take like half our tips. Just walk right into the dressing room and reach into our panties. Don't ever tell a woman to get over it."

I shrugged. "Sometimes it feels like we are speaking different languages. She speaks French and I speak Spanish, but to her there's something wrong with speaking Spanish."

"Men always think they're right. Most don't even know the word sorry. Like it would kill you to think about anything besides your thing." She looked between my legs and I quickly crossed them.

"She was trying to make me into something I wasn't. Things are problems. And problems have solutions. That's enough for me."

"What about feelings?" Boo asked. Her glass was half empty and she was having a hard time staying on the stool.

"Feelings don't solve problems. They can make you feel better about finding the answer or worse when you feel bad about not finding it. But a solution exists no matter how we feel about it. Getting upset doesn't help."

"You sound so..." she stuttered.

"Cold?" I offered. She half-nodded, half-shrugged. "I don't have much use for feelings like I don't have much use for feathers. I could have all the feathers I want and still couldn't fly. Make sense?"

"No," she said loudly.

Ed looked up from his book. He lifted the plastic bottle of cosmopolitan mix and looked at me. I nodded and he wandered down the bar with the bottle and the vodka, filling Boo's glass to the rim again. She bent over and took a drink, which was the last thing she needed.

Boo sighed like she was tired of acknowledging a universal truth, again. "Tell her men are pigs. I don't mean just you. You all want us to listen to you or give you a back rub and tell you everything will be fine. But when I want a little understanding, it's like I asked for the world."

"That's the way it used to be with Maggie and me, except I was the one saying it would all be okay. But now the joke's on us."

"What joke?"

"Maggie feels bad about me being the way I am, but she really doesn't want me to change either. She gets mad at me for making her be mad at herself. I tried to be better, to be needy. It seemed the only way I could get to feel something was to jam a pen into my thigh."

"You wouldn't want to know the things jammed in me," she muttered into her palm.

Ed came over with the bottle of Jameson's and poured without asking.

"I tried. I really did. But it was like looking for a phantom limb. It wasn't there. Maggie saw me struggling and it made her feel even worse. My daughters wondered who was this freak they have for a father. I am wearing a suit three sizes too big. I want to be graceful, but I can't help being clumsy."

"Try dancing in three-inch heels for a couple of hours if you want to know what clumsy feels like."

"But this morning I found out what real sadness feels like. My phantom limb began to hurt."

"What changed?"

"Who knows? Yesterday I had a problem I couldn't solve. A customer of mine couldn't empty his recycling bin on his desktop. It was driving him nuts. I tried everything. And nothing worked. There was a file he wanted to get rid of, but couldn't. He made me promise not to open it. I did, but he stood over my shoulder the whole time. It's still there."

"Last night I couldn't sleep. I went down to get something to drink, but ended up staring out the kitchen window at our neighbor's house—they had outlined their garbage cans in white, blinking lights. Maggie walked into the kitchen, complaining about how poorly she had slept—what was worrying her, both long and short term. What she feared the girls were becoming. How she just couldn't calm down. She just needed someone to tell her it would be fine. And I wasn't there. She got scared that something happened to me. I wasn't sure whether she was worrying about me or her.

"For once, I wanted to tell her how I woke up in a panic with something burning in my chest. She stared at me like I had come out of a pod during the night. I waited for her to say something to comfort me. But you know what she did? She flipped her hair out of her face and told me it was going to be fine. What does that mean? Fine? I wanted her to make me feel better and all she could do was pat me on the head and tell me I would feel better in the morning. We would both feel better. What she meant is I would feel better so I could stop talking about me and start making her feel better. She went back to bed, accidentally turning off the lights when she left. I have never felt so exposed, so naked."

I stopped, feeling no better for talking and then felt worse because Boo looked like she was stifling a laugh. "That's it? Your wife doesn't understand you? You know how many times I hear that in a day? Just because you had a bad day and couldn't sleep doesn't mean your life has changed forever. You people and your little sufferings; you keep looking for pity. Don't look at me for it."

She could tell she had hurt my feelings and realized that wasn't her job. Ed looked up and frowned at her like a parent silently telling a child to behave in public. Her voice was cold even though she was reaching around to remove her bra. "You want to see naked? I'll show you naked. Half-off until nine."

Five People, Not Including the Guy With a Broom

Death makes me hungry

Chorus: Only you could think about yourself at someone else's funeral.

So this is hell. Hot, crowded, loud, with no place to sit. The earnest young women with guitars are singing a set of Indigo Girls covers. As if that isn't bad enough, my personal hell also includes a large mayonnaise stain on my right thigh.

Chorus: Why did you stop for a burger?

Why did I stop for a burger? I brought lunch to work, the usual—turkey on wheat, pretzels and an apple. Healthy and filling. Just not as fulfilling as a Five Guys burger, which is where I found myself on the way to the funeral. What can I say? I'm Jewish; death makes me hungry.

The whole afternoon had the feeling of transgression. I left work early to attend the funeral of the son of a colleague. I didn't know the colleague well or her son at all. I knew he had died young, leaving a wife and a baby. How worked up could I get for people I barely knew? Don't get me wrong, I am a sensitive guy. I am just not one of those people who wears his emotions on his sleeve. Just mayonnaise on his pants. I saw the sign for Five Guys up ahead and was in the lot before I knew it. Might as well make a day of it.

Chorus: Sometimes I don't even know you.

I took some theological satisfaction in not ordering bacon on my cheeseburger, though the counter girl, Circe-like, offered twice. A guy could get dragged to his doom by those brown eyes, dimples and blonde hair pulled back into a ponytail. "No," I said, holding up a firm hand, "just a cheeseburger with lettuce, tomato, pickles, onions, ketchup and mayonnaise."

Chorus: It's still treif, including her.

You'd think God would have pity on me. But no. I had taken maybe four or five bites when I felt something tectonically shift under my fingers. And then something wet and warm landed on my slacks. I knew what had happened before I looked down and how hopeless it would be. No amount of rubbing with a shredded napkin or the carbonated water provided by the sympathetic counter girl could erase the stain or shame. I looked at my watch and realized I had less time than I thought. I tossed half of the burger and most of the fries on my way out. Circe waved and told me to come again.

The car smelled of mayonnaise and onions. What time was it? 3:40. I had 20 minutes to get to the Temple. Could I make it home and change in time? Even if I did 90 and wasn't pulled over, I would still be ten minutes late. I could imagine everyone watching me have to ask half a row of people to stand up so I can take an empty seat.

Chorus: You only have yourself to blame.

I would have to brave it and hope I was lucky enough to sit next to someone who didn't know me or had no sense of smell. I didn't want to be there too early for fear I would be dragged into a conversation with a congregant who couldn't wait to get home and tell his wife how Ross smelled like a condiment bar. I slowed down, much to the dismay of the kids in the Charger behind me. I needed to kill five minutes to arrive just in time for the mingling to end, but too late for me to make it to the front row to express my condolences to the family. I turned down a side street and made a circle before pulling into the parking lot.

Shit. It was packed! Why didn't I anticipate this? Jesus Christ, people were double parked. I looked down the street; there wasn't a free spot to be had. People dressed in black and sunglasses were making their way down the sidewalks. It looked like an alien invasion.

Chorus: If only you had driven directly to the Temple, none of this would happen.

Was this a punishment from God? No place to park and an enormous stain on my pants? No one had seen me. How hard was it to drive on and show up at shiva and pretend I was way in the back of the sanctuary? Or I could simply say something came up at work and I couldn't get away. She would believe me because I would look guilty; I already was.

An arm shot up and waved at me. Simon, of all people. Simon was the conscience of any conversation. He had this smile that reminded me of a Salem Elder who simply had a few questions to ask you as he ushered you into the dunking chair. There was something serpentine about his unblinking eye and flicking tongue. Even when I had nothing to feel guilty about, Simon was able to slip his stiletto in and strike something vital. He motioned for me to roll down my window.

"Isn't this amazing?" he asked, gesturing at the masses moving down the street.

"Uh huh," I said, "can't even find a parking spot." I was hoping he would confirm my suspicion and then give me the cover I would need to be late or not to show up at all.

But that's not what Simon does. He cheerfully told me the YMCA across the street had made an exception; there was plenty of parking to be had. "This really is something," he said, now leaning into my window. Were his nostrils flaring slightly and his tongue wagging? Was he about to ask me if a mayonnaise jar had broken in my car? But he wanted to make me feel much worse.

Chorus: I always liked Simon—a success and still a Mentsch.

"I really shouldn't be surprised that the Temple is packed. Eli was a great guy."

"He was."

"I didn't know you knew him."

Caught. "I didn't. I mean, I didn't know him well. I just heard he was a great guy."

Chorus: You would think that the foot in your mouth would stop you from talking.

"He was more than great. He was one of a kind."

"One of a kind," I repeated with little enthusiasm.

He looked at me again and shook his head as if he questioned what I had ever accomplished. Lucky for me, he was crushed by Eli's death. Recriminations had to wait. "Poor Sheila is really having a hard time."

"I imagine it is one of the worst things someone could go through."

Chorus: There are worse things. Trust me. I know.

"I can't even imagine it." Was everything a competition with him? "I don't know what I would do if something happened to one of my girls," he said, fully aware I didn't have any children. "Such a tragedy. I just hope Sheila will let me help her." Game, set and match. I hadn't even called or sent a card and he volunteered to have her outsource her life to him.

Chorus: Altruism has never been one of your traits.

"I probably shouldn't be blocking traffic," I said into the empty rear-view mirror. Apparently everybody but me knew of the YMCA's offer and were pulling into the parking lot.

"Yes, I should get back in there. Only stepped out to get my suit jacket. I didn't want to get anything on it when I was assembling shiva trays." He looked at my wrinkled dress shirt and smiled. "See you in there." I couldn't tell if that was a threat.

Chorus: Such a nice boy that Simon.

Of course I had to park on the other side of the baseball field and, looking at my watch, realized I had less than five minutes to get in. I had no choice but to run across the diamond and by the time I reached third base, my pants and shoes were covered in a fine coating of yellow dust. I looked like a car that had been abandoned years ago. Of course, the dust was attracted to the mayonnaise stain and it looked like I had a fungal growth on my pants.

Chorus: You're going to a funeral dressed like that?

My God, they had to rent a cop to direct traffic. Who was this guy? Everybody, with the exception of me, looked like they had never experienced such pain in their lives. A woman to my left, wearing a sleeveless black dress that revealed a large tiger tattoo on her right shoulder, was leaning heavily against what I assumed was her boyfriend who was wearing black jeans and a black silk shirt.

The woman at the door, who wore an usher label and looked vaguely familiar, grabbed me and drew me into an enormous hug. "It is just so sad. So sad," she said into my chest. I patted her on the head and could only come up with "yeah." I disengaged and looked into her moist eyes and told her I was sorry although I didn't know what for. She nodded in appreciation and started sniffing the air, left and right. By the time she got back to me, I was already down the hall in the middle of the herd heading into the sanctuary.

I belong to a reform temple so we were lucky if the congregation required more than three rows of seats. Only on the High Holidays would there be enough people in the room to require ventilation and the fans would belch out the dust that had accumulated since last Yom Kippur. Repentance to me is usually accompanied by itchy eyes and a runny nose.

Chorus: Maybe if you went more often you wouldn't be allergic.

But today, there wasn't a seat to be had. Across the sanctuary, I spied Mrs. Cohen in her walker, trying to sit on a loudspeaker.

I didn't even bother to look for a seat and made for the back wall to stand among the road company from the Cook County Juvenile Detention Center. The kids around me were wearing baggy pants down to their knees, loose and revealing t-shirts with obscene messages and bejeweled baseball caps pulled over their eyes. Instinctively, I moved my wallet from the back to my front pocket, much to the disapproval of a white woman with a nose ring. She rolled her eyes, "tutted" loudly and said something to the woman with the multi-colored hair, who joined in her displeasure. She looked me up and down and stopped at my fuzzy spot.

Chorus: If only you were on time, you would have a seat up front, away from the hoodlums. And you wouldn't smell of mayonnaise.

I was definitely in trouble and the skies outside darkened in concert with my mood. While I seemed ignored by everyone there who were engrossed in listening to a recording of Eddie Vedder accompanied by a tabla, this was surely a temporary condition. At any moment, I was confident five hundred pairs of eyes would turn around, consider me from head to dusty toe and ask the question that had been bugging them since I walked in: why did Eli die instead of you?

Chorus: It does seem like he was more accomplished than you. And five years younger, too.

The first speaker was a professor who taught at the same inner-city college as Eli. He had the cadence and the posture of someone who spent a considerable amount of time with young blacks. It was less a sermon than a rap and soon the audience, comprised of mostly liberal white people, were waving their arms and clapping more or less on beat. I was appalled. Not because he was comfortable impersonating a person several shades darker than himself, but because I knew I never could pull it off.

Chorus: Now you want to be a schwartse?

I consider myself to be firmly left of center. I not only voted for Obama, I had sent him twenty-five dollars. As to equality of the races, count me in. If you asked me if a black man was my equal, I would say of course with the same conviction that I would say the sun rose in the east. But ultimately what does it matter to me from which direction the sun comes up? If one morning, it peeked out from the direction of Iowa, would my life really change?

And that was my attitude towards minorities. As long as they remain equal somewhere else, fine with me. But don't talk loudly on the El using indecipherably loud slang. And, whatever you do, don't walk towards me from the opposite direction with your homies because I will cross the street.

Not only was this man not afraid of blacks, he liked them; he sought them out. He admired and learned from them and, judging by the nods of approval by the thugs around me, he was accepted by them.

My first and last inclination was to consider him a poser. I hate white people who pretend they are black. But somewhere in the middle of my indignation, I realized I was jealous. I would never be comfortable in the company of more than two black people. Imagine me trying to wear bling; it would be like a decorating a hosta and calling it a Christmas tree.

When he finished, there were whoops and hollers from the usually sedate congregation, which felt like nothing less than a thousand fingernails scraping a blackboard.

Chorus: Now there is a man with enthusiasm for life.

After Professor Homey came another white guy. I promised myself if he started rapping, I would leave. I didn't care who saw me go. There is only so much a guy can take. Besides I would garner less attention leaving than screaming.

But he didn't rap. Instead he reached into his jacket and withdrew a slip of paper and propped a pair of reading glasses onto his nose. He unfolded the paper and cleared his throat. His voice was like a faucet with a slow leak—more than a murmur, less than a whisper. Everyone in the sanctuary leaned forward, holding on to the vague hope they would know when he was done and could applaud appropriately.

Despite there being hundreds of people in the room, I had never witnessed such an exhibition of concentration. No one was moving or breathing. What would it be like to have people afford me such concentration? What would it be like for them to hang on my every word as if they were panning for gold? Even though I was all the way in the back of the room, I could feel the blood rushing to my face because I knew I could do nothing more than disappoint.

Chorus: When important people talk, people listen.

The rabbi came over and pushed the microphone into his face and he muttered an apology and started over again. He explained he was Eli's editor and would like to share something with us that Eli had just completed two weeks earlier. He stopped and looked like he had been caught lying. He said he was less Eli's editor than Eli's admirer. Because being an editor implied he edited Eli's work. Eli rarely needed editing. In his opinion, he had never read a writer who was able to convey his meaning in such clear and simple words.

"What Eli was about was conveying big ideas (very big ideas) in small quiet words. And this," he said, holding up the piece of paper, "is full of very big ideas. Ideas that the world may never ever see again."

Chorus: Such a shame.

He stopped talking and looked up at the dark sky in the windows above me. What did he see? Eli, floating in the clouds, or a vengeful God about to strike me down? He started to cry. I don't mean merely tears streaming down his cheek, but shoulder-shaking, nose-running weeping. I have seen children ripped away from their parents by Protective Services blubber less.

No one moved. Shouldn't someone hug him or help him back to his seat? We just watched this man cry in front of hundreds of strangers. It was unbearable. Not only because I was embarrassed for him, but because I knew no one, especially an editor, would care if I died.

Chorus: I would care. Not that you would care if I cared.

For as long as I can remember I have always wanted to be a writer. I, too, had big ideas raging in my mind. I would stare into the mirror as a child, trying to look deep. The world was simply waiting for me to put pen to paper and illuminate the darkness. Early poems were simply screeds about how dark everything seemed and how frustrated I was that I could not find the light.

Chorus: I found your poems once. They were next to those dirty pictures you hid under your mattress.

While my ideas were prodigious, the words to describe them were not. Each word had to be coaxed out of a cave. A drowsy adjective would stumble out, rubbing its eyes, and stare reluctantly at me. Looking down, I realized it was wrong and sent it back into the cave. The process repeated until what I thought what was the right-sounding word slumped out. He would look at me, disappointed to have been chosen by such an obvious minor-league talent. We hoped to develop some sort of affinity for each other. I might as well have hoped to fall in love with my dental hygienist. Both cases would cause equal amounts of discomfort and incoherence.

Chorus: Poor little word. It just breaks your heart.

What I eventually discovered was I had the desire to write, but not the talent. While the ideas flitted around my head like butterflies, as soon as they were set free, they might as well have been a moth to an interstate windshield.

But not Eli. He had both the ideas and the talent. So much so that revealing them after his death was too painful. Fortunately for me, the rabbi took pity on the editor and wrapped an experienced arm around his shoulder and guided him back to his seat. Who the hell was he to set us up and then "claim" he was too overcome with emotion to share the best thing ever written? I bet it wasn't. I bet he took another look at the first pages and realized he was mistaken. But I knew that wasn't it. The purpose wasn't to share, it was to make me feel even worse.

Chorus: Always about you. Always.

So what was I left with? A feeling of emptiness and knowing there was a work of genius I would never write. I would grow old and, if I was lucky to find someone to marry a man in his late thirties, and if we would be able to have children, what was the best I could expect? A lingering death like my mother's. The only saving grace was I would not have to witness the embarrassment of watching my son finding my collected writings and the porn I forgot to delete.

I imagined his face, at first joyful to find what could be a treasure trove of unpublished work that he could publish in act of filial duty and/or personal gain. I would be spared his fading enthusiasm as he read story after story and found nothing more than a series of self-flagellating lamentations masquerading as fiction. I saw him slowly shaking his head as he found nothing of worth and wondered how his father could be so deluded. I watched his finger on the delete button, going up and down with the speed of an experienced telegraph operator, file after file is consigned to the other side of history. He smiled as he shut down the computer for the final time, knowing he has spared my memory and himself of any potential embarrassment.

Chorus: At least you had a child who knew better than to air his dirty laundry in public.

How long could the funeral last? I certainly wasn't going to stay for the reception afterwards. I couldn't force anything down my constricted throat and expect it to stay in my stomach.

I looked at my watch. Over an hour had gone by since I had arrived. Standing over an hour on one's feet, surrounded by the cast of *West Side Story* and having all your flaws pointed out to you seems like ample penance. That counts as an expression of sympathy, doesn't it?

I smiled at Simon who had a pitcher of ice water in one hand and plastic glasses in the other. He raised an eyebrow as if he was chiding me for not serving our guests.

I couldn't wait to seethe in the privacy of my condo. I had it all planned out—an Italian Beef from the pizza place, a couple beers and whatever soft-core I had Tivo'ed on Cinemax. The way I was feeling, screw the cholesterol and the dubious ethics of masturbating instead of attending shiva. I couldn't feel any worse.

Chorus: Maybe if you applied yourself.

I was, of course, sadly mistaken. I looked up and saw Sheila slowly making her way up to the pulpit. She had aged ten years in the last week. She was somewhere in her sixties, but it was an ageless sixty, wearing bright dresses and loud bracelets. Even though her hair had turned grey a long time ago, it was the silver grey that was more stylish than old. But now her hair had turned yellow and hung about her shoulders like it, too, was burdened by unbearable sadness. She shuffled slowly up the stairs, never letting go of the handrail on one side and her youngest daughter on the other. The rabbi and cantor met her at the top and each gave her a sustained and sustaining hug. She looked like she would collapse if they released her too quickly.

Chorus: Mothers know suffering and children know how to cause it.

"Oh Christ," I said, loudly. At least five pairs of eyes, some hidden behind crystal studded sunglasses, regarded me with disbelief and disapproval. I wasn't being sardonic. I was being perspicacious. I knew what was to come. My whole body stiffened and something heavy and tight was moving its way from my stomach up my throat. My eyes were moist and would let go with the slightest provocation.

The provocation came with her reaching into her pocket to unfold a small piece of paper. Her daughter stood behind her, barely able to keep herself erect. They looked like women of Troy, regarding the ruins that had been their lives.

Sheila began to speak softly. I could only make out every other word. But I knew exactly what she was saying. It was not because I was familiar with the words of a grieving mother, because I was not. Everything she said about Eli could be applied to me so long as the words "not, never or even once" were affixed to the head of the sentence.

Chorus: Not, never or even once.

It wasn't so much of a eulogy as the cutting of a diamond. She had this wonderful gem in her life and was happy with it as it was. But as he grew into the man he would become, she discovered more—his humor, his love of music, his compassion, his love of his sisters and family. Each discovery added brilliance to his life and to hers.

As he grew he shed the parts of him that may have been attractive at first, but, with the cutter's expert eye, were extraneous and cut them away without fear or loss. Gone were his temper, his impatience, his petty jealousies. And with their jettisoning, came even more brilliance, the woman who would become his wife, the son who caused his heart to expand and the kids from Englewood and Austin to whom he gave voice and confidence.

Chorus: And you have accomplished exactly what?

She looked at all the people who loved Eli and realized there were so many more facets to her son she never suspected. She had always loved Eli so deeply. But now she felt cheated that she would never know him fully.

She felt like walking up to each person and asking them to tell her about Eli, how he had touched them and what they knew about them. She would gather up these stories and memories and take them out one by one on cold winter days so she could be comforted by this son whose warmth she barely comprehended.

Chorus: There's no bottom to a mother's pain.

She stopped as if she was drowning and just barely made it to the surface to take a breath of air before being dragged under again. It would never be enough to make her forget the pain his death will cause her every day for the rest of her life. These would only be stories and memories. They wouldn't be Eli. You can't hold on tightly to stories and memories. No story would ever come for Shabbes dinner and fall asleep on the couch. No memory would fill her empty condo any more.

She had been robbed of a son whom she loved dearly and no matter how many times she told him how much she loved him and was so proud of him, it wasn't enough. If only she could hold his hand like a child crossing the street. This time he wouldn't need to walk. She would sweep him up into her arms and never let him go. Never let him go away.

She turned away from the microphone and fell into her daughter's chest. There wasn't a dry eye in the sanctuary, especially mine. I was not crying because it was Eli's funeral but because of the overwhelming feeling that it could never be my funeral. The one I would never have. It was too late. What ever road I should have taken, I lost my way a long time ago.

There would be no celebration of my kindness, my talent, my warm heart. There would be no singing or even crying. There would be no throngs of people. If I was lucky, there would be five people at my funeral, including the guy with the broom.

Chorus: If you are lucky.

Alice and Angus

WK/RT

Cheryl clamped her hand over the phone and said, "It's Alice. Be nice. She just wants to talk to you." Her face was flushed, clearly expecting me to do something stupid. Given that my nineteen-year-old daughter was on the line, the likelihood that I would was high.

I looked up from my Sunday *New York Times*. Since Alice had gone to college, it was my weekly pleasure to read the *Times* and drink coffee in the Florida room. Before then, Alice demanded our attention, whether it was to drive her to recitals or sleepovers or fight over a dirty bedroom or the clothing she distributed throughout the house. When she was even younger, she required me to do puzzles with her, build Lego castles and change endless diapers. Whatever the reason, the Sunday *Times* usually sat unopened on the piano in the living room, waiting to be recycled. And now Alice was disturbing my pleasure via long distance.

I flipped the paper down and looked at Cheryl. "How much is it going to cost?"

Cheryl sighed a practiced groan. For most of Alice's life, she had been the intermediary between Alice and me. Cheryl always had more patience with Alice's high-strung personality and was not averse to reading me the riot act when I would strategically leave military academy pamphlets on her desk. Even though Alice would try Cheryl's patience, she was ashamed that I often wished aloud for a condom the night we conceived Alice. We could have tried another time when calmer sperm would prevail. I did not hate her, Cheryl explained to the both of us, I was just tired.

Cheryl held the phone out to me as if she was threatening me with it. "Just talk to her," and then added, "and listen."

"Hello, Alice," I said as if I were expecting the voice of doom on the other end.

"Hi, Dad," Alice's voice was bright and seemed completely unaware of our long and combative history. "I've got great news for you."

"Really?" Cheryl looked at me with disappointment and left the room. I tried to alter my tone, but it was like altering the Titanic's course. "What's the great news?"

"I went to the AC/DC concert last night. Guess who I slept with?"

I felt the familiar emotion of wondering whom she was allowing to despoil her. It was worse now there was confirmation. Someone had touched her. Someone she met at an AC/DC concert. I saw spots on the wall and the receiver dangled precariously in my fingers.

"Who?" was all I could manage.

She sounded as if she had found a kitten. "Angus Young."

The name was familiar, but would not register. Angus Young was probably some pimply face teenager who passed her a joint and then lured her into the back of his parent's Buick. "Who?" I asked again.

This time she sounded disappointed as if I had told her she couldn't keep the kitty. "Angus Young, Dad, of AC/DC? You know, Angus."

I felt a wave of nausea break over me as I began to process this information. I had never had a heart attack, but I was pretty sure I was having one—vertigo, chest pains and supreme confusion. When I spoke, my voice sounded like it was coming from the bottom of a sewer. "You slept with Angus Young?"

"I did! It was so awesome!" Had she forgotten to whom she was speaking? Maybe she hit the wrong button on her phone.

What I would give to forget the whole thing—to erase the image of some sweaty middle-aged pervert with bad teeth half out of a schoolboy outfit rutting my daughter. I am not one to be willfully ignorant, but in this case, I was willing to give it a try.

"You slept with Angus Young?" Please say no. Please say no.

Alice was undeterred. "Dad, it's true. I thought you would be excited for me."

"You thought I would be excited for you? You actually think I would be happy that some senior citizen took advantage of you?"

"Dad, he's not a senior citizen. He's not even sixty yet. And he didn't take advantage of me. I came on to him. I even had to show him my license to prove I was over eighteen."

"Chivalry isn't dead, apparently."

"He was a gentleman. He was much more gentle than you would suspect. Not at all how he is on stage."

"Alice, I really don't feel comfortable having this conversation with you. But keep going, because I am pretty sure a massive coronary is about to hit, taking me out of my misery."

"Dad, will you chill? You were the one who told me that you could make love to the guitar riffs at the beginning of 'Back in Black.'"

"It was Malcolm who played that riff. And I was joking."

"So I made a mistake. Sue me."

"I should say so. What were you thinking? Oh, I forgot, you weren't. Thinking about consequences is so old-fashioned, isn't it?"

"Quit it, Dad. You sound like Nana."

"Maybe for once your grandmother and I agree."

"Well, it's done, so get over it. Really, I thought you would be happy for me."

"You did? You really thought I would be happy that you slept with Angus Young? Who are you?"

It was a question floating around in my mind since the moment Alice was born. As Cheryl pushed one last time and Alice popped into this world, I waited for a rush of white-hot love for my first born. I expected to be overwhelmed by the moment. I wanted to feel something incredible that happened. But I didn't. All I saw was me holding my infant daughter, waiting for me to love her more than anything else in the world. Imagine her disappointment when I couldn't.

That night as I slept in a chair by Cheryl's bed, I watched the two of them nuzzle as if they didn't need anyone else in the world, including me. It got worse the moment Alice cried for the first time. Not having productive breasts, I was powerless to do anything about it.

Every howl proved I was not cut out for fatherhood. She was barely five hours old when I tried to soothe her unsuccessfully and felt the resentment and the anger arise, like some sort of perverse afterbirth. I squeezed her and shook her, but she didn't get any quieter. I felt completely impotent. I stared out in the darkness, waiting for Cheryl to wake up and take Alice. But she slept on.

Friends and family came and went, all declaring Alice's beauty and my luck. I didn't notice either.

Alice had my number from the beginning. She squinted at me with newborn grey-green eyes, accusing me of merely impersonating a father. She refused to be comforted by me, crying even louder as my fingers tightened around her little thighs. "Shut up, Alice, shut up," I whispered between clenched teeth, trying to figure out the line between rocking a child and shaking it.

There weren't eleven words that struck more fear in my heart than Cheryl saying, "I'm going out for a couple hours, can you watch Alice?" I would tiptoe by Alice's room, hoping that she would spend the entire time asleep in her crib.

She never did. Cheryl would be gone not five minutes when I would hear Alice stirring in her crib, utterly sweet guttural coos, a sign that she believed Cheryl was still in the house. But for me they were like the rustling of leaves, signaling an unseasonable blizzard. I would freeze, not breathing, praying that she was only stirring mid-dream.

When Cheryl did not arrive to rub her back, Alice realized she was alone with me. Like the wind out of the Rockies, she began to wail. Louder and louder, as she expelled discontent from her lungs. Why did she do this? She knew her cries cut straight through me and gnawed at my greatest insecurities. And the more I hurt, the more I wanted to hurt her. I would pick her up, put her down, change her, feed her, comfort her, but nothing seemed to work. What did she want from me?

Eventually, I would leave her in the crib alone and hide in the garage until I heard Cheryl pulling into the driveway. And then I walked out at the same moment that Cheryl walked in the door. I shrug my shoulders and tell Cheryl I hadn't heard Alice crying. Holding up my oily hands and I told Cheryl that I'd get her as soon as I washed my hands. Cheryl waved me off, instructing me to put away whatever she had just bought.

It seemed hopeless to me. I realized parenthood had been a mistake; the best I could hope for was a quick childhood and the human equivalent of treeing Alice when she was old enough to fend for herself. Of course, I kept this plan secret and made daily promises to keep my head down and my temper in check. I looked at my four-month-old daughter and offered a truce—if she didn't bother me, I wouldn't bother her.

A miracle occurred when Alice was about ten months old. Selfishly, Cheryl had made a haircut appointment on a Saturday (she usually did so on her lunch hour so our babysitter would be watching Alice). To make matters worse, she had also made a lunch date with her best friend, Theresa. Just the two of them at the mall, no kids. I would be lucky if they were back by St. Patrick's Day.

Two sets of nose prints, one high and one low, were on the patio door as Cheryl backed out of the driveway. Alice and I looked at each other with distaste and distrust.

I placed Alice in the playroom and surrounded her with a collection of stuffed animals, blocks, books, and pillows. I was hoping she wouldn't notice that her playpen resembled a prison. I told her Daddy would be working in the living room and to call me if she needed me. I went into the living room, slipped in AC/DC's "Dirty Deeds Done Dirt Cheap" and turned the volume to seven. Every glass and window and the house shook to Malcolm's riffs.

I did not notice Alice until she had used my right pant leg as a climbing support. She was learning to walk and she must have crawled all the way from the playroom, past her bedroom, the kitchen, the dining room, and down the three stairs that led to the living room. If I hadn't been annoyed at being disturbed, I would have been impressed. I picked her up and was about to march her back to the playroom when she looked up at me with luminous eyes, smiled at me for the first time in her life and said, "Duhty dees?"

I suppose it should have been more meaningful to me if her first words were "Dada," but somehow I felt a connection akin to what Cheryl felt all along. They say mothers are bound to their children emotionally and physically and that fathers have to find their own way. Most are simply nice guys who assume the connection and never question it. Others are like me who figure that the best we can do is fake it.

But looking into my daughter's eyes as she repeated, "Duhty dees," I felt something new and alien stirring in me. It reminded me of the Grinch's heart expanding and bursting through the confines of a hardened hedge. Cheryl hated AC/DC. She called it my teenage stoner music and it became my pornography, only brought out when she was not around.

But what if I had been mistaken? What if it had all been a cruel joke? Some sort of pulling the rug out from under me? What if it weren't a father-daughter moment—it was gas?

I picked Alice up and walked over to the stereo. I hit the review button on the CD player and off Malcolm went again. It didn't take three notes of the opening riff for the heavens to open up and God's grace to shine on my daughter and me. A smile came over her face and illuminated me. "Duhty dees," she laughed, "duhty dees!" She clapped her little hands together in a way that Barney could never move her. "Duhty dees!"

"You want some dirty deeds?" I asked her, doing my best Bon Scott impersonation. I deposited her next to the metal radiator cover and returned to the stereo. I hit review again and turned the stereo up. The windows began to shiver and I am sure that outside it sounded as if someone was tossing grenades inside.

The noise was truly painful, but Alice just laughed. I helped her steady herself on her feet and began to pound on the radiator cover with my hands, adding to the racket. Alice, banging her little hands, shouted, "Duhty dees duhty dees."

Outside a neighbor was building a snowman with his two children, a wholesome Norman Rockwell scene. He was doing his best to ignore the Sodom and Gomorrah inside my house.

Alice and I regarded each other suspiciously at first, a toddler and her parent realizing there was a circuitous way out of the hell we would find ourselves in for the next eighteen years. Soon we were laughing and pounding to the beat. We didn't hear Cheryl come in and we certainly did not hear her equate the ear-bleeding music with child abuse. Cheryl shut off the stereo, which was okay because Alice and I were exhausted. That night, I tucked Alice into her crib and kissed her forehead warmly. She opened one eye and whispered, "Duhty dees," and fell asleep with a smile on her face.

But what we found was not Nirvana, but more like an oasis. More than a mirage, less than a destination. Alice awoke with a shriek. She had peed through her diaper and I spent the better part of the morning wringing cold urine out of the bedding. When I started singing AC/DC as a way to placate her, she looked insulted. Was it because I was not Bon Scott or because I thought things would be easy from now on?

Alice and I coexisted through the remainder of her childhood. On good days, when I had a successful day at work and Alice had not gotten into a fight in school, we would pop in a CD and discuss the merits of Bon Scott (impish and care-free) versus Brian Johnson (guttural and street). We would listen to the opening chimes of "Hell's Bells" as if we were listening to the chimes of Westminster.

Bon's death became a metaphor for our relationship. On bad days, when Cheryl, Alice, and Babs, the cat, all seemed to be aligned against me, I would whisper about too many women and too many pills. Alice would look at me with the same skeptical stare and tell me that my life had never been that exciting.

It would be a lie to say that I did not love Alice. I am pretty sure I would have stepped in front of a truck to save her. But I am also equally sure that the last thing to go through my mind before the truck's grill would be, "Thanks a lot, Alice."

So what was it with Alice that drove me nuts? Well, there was her constant obsession with herself, whether it was her knowledge or her looks. Even as a little girl, she regarded me as an idiot. She might not be wrong, but couldn't she keep a secret? She was the only kid I knew who would stare at you with doubt before you could get out, "Because I said so."

AC/DC remained our safe harbor. We had most of the essential albums on CD and at any moment we could have popped one into the stereo, but the real joy came when an AC/DC song came on the radio, like the sun breaking through the clouds. Playing a CD to promote détente was equivalent to cheating, akin to watching a tape of a "Charlie Brown Christmas" in July. One can only fake emotion so far.

But that does not mean we did not put ourselves in the position to be surprised by happenstance. Once after a particular vicious fight about how utterly insensitive I was to her harpy-like emotions, I turned on the radio in the kitchen to drown out Alice's shrieks as she tried to explain to Cheryl my location on the pantheon of evil parents.

I was hoping for the NPR station, but instead stumbled on a small low wattage station out of Joliet. The DJs seemed to be under both the age of twenty and the influence. Something was hysterical, but they weren't sharing. There was the sound of fumbling about and then I heard the lush and unmistakable strains of Malcolm sliding down the neck of his Gretch.

"Alice," I called, running into her bedroom. I ignored their spiteful looks and grabbed Alice by the wrist and dragged her downstairs to the kitchen. Cheryl screamed and Alice tried to get away. I remained determined, as I had to get Alice into the kitchen before Bon crooned of his favorite type of balls, the ones held for pleasure.

Alice cocked her ear. Her shoulders, which had been tense like those of a lioness about to pounce, relaxed. An easy smile came to her face as she listened to a bevy of double entendres. She was clearly enjoying herself and, as a result of being the author of her happiness, I was also happy. "You see. You see," I said to her, demonstrating I wasn't the ogre she thought I was. Maybe she had been wrong about me. And perhaps through self-awareness, she would come to realize that she isn't always right. I smiled paternalistically at her.

But Alice jutted out her still child-sized chin but in a voice well beyond her age, she claimed to have the biggest balls of all. Even though I was a good head taller than she, it was unnerving to face down the pre-teen stare. I know Alice was joking, but I wasn't in the mood to be laughed at. I wanted a connection, not attitude.

At that moment, I had a choice either to be a child abuser or an ineffective parent. Either way, I was pretty sure I would be blamed or at least at fault for the many times that Alice would stray from the path. And in whatever ditch she ended up, there would be evidence leading directly back to this moment.

I felt my fingers coil into a fist as if they had made the decision for me. In my mind, I could see her right cheek, already reddening from the blow, turning away from me as she fell to the floor. I saw the look of hatred and unwillingness to forgive. But then Bon interrupted with talk of seafood cocktail and crabs.

Alice and I never found a consistent rhythm throughout her teen years. They were awful and corresponded to the worst five years of my professional career. There is nothing worse than going to a job you detest and to have it seasoned with the fear of being handed a box and five minutes to clean up your desk. I made it through the day (barely) and then realized that I had survived another day just to come home to a battlefield.

By the time she turned fifteen, Alice had declared war on nearly everyone. Childhood friends were discarded as carelessly as the granola bar wrappers she left strewn all over the house. Alice was given the gift of an able tongue, which she sharpened on a daily basis. And while her oratorical skills had progressed, her ability to control them regressed until the point that a two-year-old would be impressed by her tantrums.

Even Cheryl became a target of Alice's assaults. I once came home to find Cheryl, wine glass grasped tightly in hand, sitting at the kitchen table looking at the backyard fence as if she was contemplating escape. I didn't have to ask, but I did to make sure the evening had already been ruined. "Alice?"

Cheryl nodded and drained the glass. I could see her fingers grasping the bowl so tightly; it was amazing it did not shatter.

"You want me to talk to her?" I knew the answer, but some things you do for the sheer comfort that accompanies futility.

Cheryl looked at me from beneath red-rimmed eyes and smirked. "You do and you'll win the Nobel Peace Prize."

Walking up stairs, I considered Alice's closed door, which was metaphor enough without the post-it note pasted above the doorknob on which was written "Private—keep out." I sighed and searched the meager resources of my parental lobe for an appropriate approach. But all I heard was static and I walked into my bedroom to get changed. I smirked at my reflection in the mirror; nothing made me feel more impotent than parenthood.

Absentmindedly, I turned on the clock radio by my bed. The two and half-inch speaker did no justice to "Highway to Hell," but it did attract Alice's attention. She was wearing an old oxford shirt and tube socks she had expropriated from me. Her hair was a gnarled mess and her eyes were dewy. As pathetic a vision as she presented, she still intimidated me. I took one or two involuntary steps backwards. Alice pressed in closer.

"Nice try," she said, with all the warmth of an assassin.

I was oblivious to what she meant. It took me a few seconds and actually listening to the chorus to figure out what she talking about. "You give me too much credit, kitten," I told her. "I just switched it on."

"Yeah," she said, dragging her fingers through her hair (which she did when frustrated), "my mistake."

"I'm too tired to fight. Nothing I can say is going to make a difference. You can either sit here with me and listen or you can go back to your room. I wish I could do more, but I can't." I sat with my back to her. I couldn't tell if she was staying, leaving, or about to plunge a knife in my neck.

I felt the bed depress next to me. We did not make eye contact, both simply staring at the closet door. Sitting in absolute silence while Bon shrieked. The song was over and replaced by something terrible from REO Speedwagon. Instinctively, father and daughter reached to turn off the radio. Our hands met on the way. Ever the gentleman, I let her move the switch. But she grabbed my hand and put it on the bed between us. It remained there, entwined with hers for a few moments.

"You hate me, don't you?" she said quietly.

"No, I don't hate you." I wasn't lying.

"You don't like me very much, though."

I sighed, shaking my head. "No, not really. But it isn't all your fault." It was one of those moments that I wished I could take back. "I'm sorry," I said, not because I had said something that I didn't mean, but because I meant it. Why didn't I simply lie? Tell her I liked her?

I could feel Alice stiffen and her hand felt like lead in mine. I guessed she was crying. But I felt like it would be intruding to comfort her. All I could do is be next to her. We might as well have been two strangers on a bus. The girl crying next to me could be mourning a relationship that had ended or was running away from an abusive father and I, the man with the newspaper, felt sympathy for her, but turned up the volume on my iPod. Soon, I would get off the bus and walk the short distance to my life and this girl would travel on the way to her private hell. We sat for a few moments more and she stood up and went back to her room. I was thankful for small favors.

Alice and I stayed out of each other's way. I left for work before she got up and often found myself working late. I was at birthday parties and high school graduation. But I was there more as a friend of the family.

Cheryl tried to intervene, but she eventually gave up when she came to realize that neither side wanted a resolution. It was never bad between Alice and me. We had come to realize the limits of our relationship and understood there was nothing to be done.

The only bright spot remained the occasional AC/DC song played on the radio. But as the '80s turned to '90s, the band was becoming more obscure and we heard their songs less often. We lived our separate lives like two ghosts occupying the same spot. Haunted by regret, but prevented by physics from ever truly communicating.

But when our little Joliet radio station would bestow on us "Thunderstruck" or "T.N.T.," Alice and I would jump around the kitchen, bedroom or living room like two stoned metal heads. A wooden spoon would be Angus's Gibson in Alice's hand and I would usually grab the broom and be staid Malcolm, proudly watching his younger sibling take the lead. Cheryl, who had grayed so quickly, would come and watch our impromptu concerts, smiling like an old, Scottish grandmother watching the sun set over the hills of Brigadoon, knowing full well that as soon as the song was over, the magic would be over and we would be two sour people, father and daughter, putting back our spoon and broom.

I don't want you to think I was happy with the status quo. I am pretty sure that Alice wasn't either. Every so often we would test the waters of our relationship. I would take her out to dinner as a teenager and we would sit across from each other in the booth like the worst possible blind date. We smiled politely and tried to remember not to check our watches too often. The idea was to always have something in our mouths or look expectantly for the waiter so we can tell him that everything was fine, just fine. And perhaps we could convince ourselves it was, even if we were just talking about the burgers.

Eventually, the golden day arrived that I had mentally circled on my subconscious calendar—Alice was moving out and going to college. She had been accepted to the University of Illinois, which she had chosen in a rare moment of selflessness over a private, and much more expensive, school. I nearly skipped with joy, as we made run after run to Target.

Alice seemed overjoyed as well and we had not gotten along so well since WXRT had an AC/DC marathon in the late '90s. We finished each other's sentences and laughed like friends. Cheryl seemed relieved and would have been happy had she not been afflicted by nostalgia. Her little girl had grown up, to which I answered hallelujah.

We loaded the Audi with everything she would need from now until Thanksgiving, a whole three months away! As mile after mile slipped away I found myself feeling lighter and lighter. I had done it. I had raised a child and, while the results were not pretty, I had done it. The wall I placed around myself to protect against guilt was coming down.

The Audi was the result of spending most of the money I saved for reform school tuition. I had earned it and no more would I have to worry about the deleterious effects that Alice had had on the cars we drove. No more spilled formula, juice, crackers, pretzels, cheese, yogurt and the occasional half-smoked joint that would roll out from underneath the back seat. No more dents caused by aggressive shopping carts, curbs, or parked cars that

Alice swore had not been there before she just "glanced" down to change the radio.

I switched on the radio, curious to test out the satellite radio that had come with the car as a three-month trial. Most of the stations were crap—religious nonsense, country-fried pap, hip hop, non-stop talk, obscure sports, and traffic reports from cities I had no interest in visiting. But somewhere in the middle third of the "dial," I stumbled across a familiar six staccato drumbeats followed by heart-throbbing guitar riffs and then a growl about troubles with a high school head. I could see the smile blossom on Alice's face, mirroring my own.

The radio said: AC/DC Radio and the slow realization came over me, what an epiphany must feel like. What if satellite radio had existed when Alice was growing up? We would have had nothing but 24-hour AC/DC. The only variable would have been what song they decided to play. I thought back to all the songs that would have ended arguments. It would have been like we had discovered the Rosetta Stone and could now communicate.

I looked into the rearview mirror; Alice was staring back at me with her sad, gray eyes. She was thinking the same thing. Suddenly reflected in the mirror weren't the accusing eyes of a sadist, but rather the disappointed eyes of a man, who realized it was too late to be a father of a little girl. No matter what role I would play in her life from now on, we would never get that time back. All because she had had been born eighteen years too early. I spun the volume up and let Bon tell us how it is a long way to the top. For the rest of the trip down, we just let the boys do the talking for us. Cheryl was kind enough to ignore the din.

It didn't take us long to unpack Alice into her dorm room. I think she had been preparing for this day for the past couple years. She had gotten her wish. We would leave her alone. Cheryl cried and extracted promises to be careful and stay in touch. I could not come up with anything to say except that I loved her. We found our arms would not obey our minds' command to let go. Were we making up for lost hugs? Finally, I pulled her ear close to my mouth. I felt her body go limp as she expected an apology, an admission of guilt or unconditional love. But all I could offer was one word, spoken quietly at first and then louder: "Angus. Angus. Angus."

Alice pulled away and looked like she was about to hit me. But then she smiled and kissed me on the cheek. "See ya, Dad," and she went in to her dorm room, seemingly uninterested in watching us drive away.

I stood staring at the wooden door between Alice and me. Why had I been such a jerk for all those years? What if, as Alice always insisted, it had been all my fault? She was the child and I was the parent. Why had I been so impatient? Why couldn't I, like I had counseled her a thousand times, count to ten before I said anything? I wondered if she, separated by no more than two inches, was thinking about me. A single tear rolled down my cheek.

The warmth that I had for my now-absent daughter lasted only from the moment I dropped her off at college until the moment she told me she slept with a rock guitarist, old enough to be me.

And this time, the combined strength of XM-Sirius was not enough to resurrect my faith in my daughter's ability to be anything but a disappointment to me. "Jesus, Alice, I don't know what to say. Did you at least make him wear protection?"

"Dad, how stupid do you think I am?"

"I don't think this is a good time to ask me that question."

"Is that all you are going to say?"

"Right now, yes. Is there anything else you want to tell me? Anything else that could ruin my day?"

Alice seemed genuinely upset and surprised. I could tell she was trying not to cry. "I thought you would be proud."

"You thought I would be proud? Do you even know who I am? Because I don't know who you are." She hung up and all I was left was dead air and vertigo.

"Well, you handled that well," Cheryl said into the receiver. Apparently she had listened on another extension.

"Don't start on me. There is no way you can tell me that you approve of her sleeping with Angus."

"How do you know she slept with him?"

"Weren't you listening? She said so."

"And you believed her?"

"Why wouldn't I?"

"And you're sure AC/DC was in Champaign last night?"

"How the hell would I know?"

"They were in Atlanta. I checked. Long way to go for a booty run if you ask me."

Caring

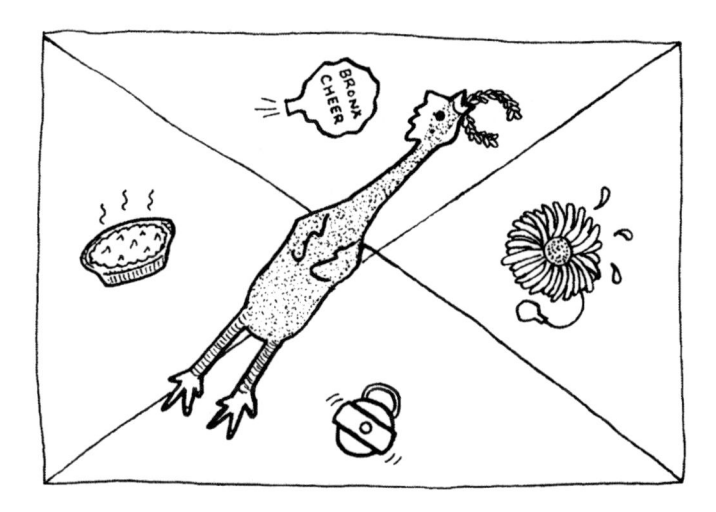

He wore a threadbare jacket over a gray argyle sweater. His bald head sported a laurel of gray, wiry hair. Enormous plastic-framed glasses perched on his broad nose like a vulture. And he was holding a pot with a tiny bonsai tree in it. Even though I was locked in the room with him, he didn't seem to notice or care.

On the flag above his head, instead of an eagle or some suitable heroic bird, there was a rubber chicken with a laurel leaf in its beak. Surrounding the chicken was, from left to right, top to bottom: a cream pie, a whoopee cushion, a squirting daisy and a hand buzzer. Ellie would be appalled.

According to Ellie, I am a jerk who doesn't care about anyone but me. She says I need to give back. I say no one has given me anything so I have nothing to give back. She replies I have been given opportunities others have not. I say I have taken advantage of opportunities that were available to anyone with half a brain.

Ellie is consumed by guilt brewed in the cauldron of our upper middle-class lives. She volunteers at a shelter, serves on the Meals on Wheels board, goes on walks with Muddles, our puggle, on behalf of the ASCPA and tutors a young mother from Pilsen at the library. It is not my fault she feels guilty. I sleep like a baby.

She told me I have to do good in this world. I asked her to define good, hoping it meant donating a Frisbee or two to a youth organization so I could be home in time to watch the Hawks game. Ellie knows my gift of finding the easiest way out of things that require me to care. She gave me two criteria to qualify as doing good: one, it must be a recognized 501(c)3 organization, and two, I must serve on the board.

I imagined an office with peeling paint and urine-soaked clients wandering about, looking for empties on the table. I promised to do my best, which we both knew would be uninspiring.

I was surprised by the paucity of choices that didn't require me to do or give much. It was amazing how many dreary causes there were—cancer, poverty, domestic abuse, drug addiction and just general malaise—that felt themselves worthy of my money and time.

I gave up and asked Alex, my secretary, to do the research that met my strict requirements—little or no contribution would be involved and I didn't have to give a damn. She had worked for me too long to be disturbed by my callousness. She placed three file folders on my desk—red, yellow and green. "As far as I can tell, none of these groups will tax your brain, wallet, or conscience."

"I'll be the judge of that," I said, and picked up the first folder. "The Fort Dearborn Massacre Foundation commemorates the massacre of white settlers by Potawatomi Indians in 1812." The rest seemed to be a catalogue of the Indians' savagery and the meek and confused reaction of the settlers who simply wanted to take the Potawatomi's land. "Who the fuck cares? That was two hundred years ago. We won. They lost. Move on, right?"

Next was the Invisible Wall Arts Center; its information brochure was a paper bag on which a description of the organization was written with a red Sharpie. Was it an invisible wall or no wall at all? Was it obvious or merely stupid? I found the answer in the second paragraph—the invisible wall is the dividing line between actor and audience. That explains it. It's stupid.

I was down to my last choice. I opened the red file and pulled out a brochure in the shape of a whoopee cushion. On the cover was: "The Fun-dation: Because it was funny." The Fundation provided micro-loans to underwrite the costs of practical jokes, pranks and non-criminal scams.

I read on. "Humor is what separates people from animals and there is no greater tragedy than a joke deferred for lack of funds." The IRS allowed them to get away with this? This was indeed the land of opportunity.

I pulled out a sheet of paper that had been photocopied many times. My heart skipped a beat just as it does when I find a dying company that can be sucked dry for profit. All I had to do was show up for one board meeting per year. There was no annual contribution or asking friends for money. All they wanted was a warm body. I was overqualified. This was a non-profit I could get behind. No smelly people missing limbs. No kids with helmets. And it wouldn't cost me a dime.

When I reported to Ellie, she offered her familiar disappointed expression.

"Spare me the look. I admit I am not a caring person. I never pretended to be. Some people can play the violin. Some people can run real fast. They have been given a gift and they make the most of it. You never look down on those who have tin ears or are slow. But if you are born without the ability to care, everyone shakes his head at you like there is something wrong with you. I am the way God made me."

"He must not have been paying attention that day," Ellie mumbled.

"Take it up with Him. My first meeting is next Tuesday. And remember, a joke is a terrible thing to waste."

The meeting was held on the twenty-fourth floor of a building that renovation forgot; the lobby was smelly, the elevators balky. The foundation offices were behind a nondescript frosted glass door with "Fun-dation (private)", painted on with peeling letters. The hallway reeked of mold and dust.

I rapped my knuckles on the glass, nearly knocking it in. A buzzer buzzed and the lock clicked like the brittle bones of an eighty-year-old. The hinges groused as the door opened, revealing a small waiting room with two chairs flanking a coffee table. A clock radio, flashing 12:00, was precariously perched on a stack of old cooking and celebrity magazines. Opposite was a wooden door with a nickel-colored handle that refused to move. I knocked on the door three times and put my ear to the door. I could hear the sound of radiators hissing, but nothing else.

I sat on the chair closest to the door and slid out a People Magazine from May 17, 2004, when the internal door opened and a heavy-set black woman appeared, wearing a flowered blouse, purple pants with ruffles at the cuffs and open-toed shoes.

She was bald. Not bald as in having thinning hair; bald as in having nothing but scalp. Behind her enormous plastic-framed glasses, there were no hints of eyebrows or lashes. Cancer, I thought. She obviously owned a tight-fitting hat as half-way up her brow was a thin furrow that ringed her head like a halo.

"Yes," she said, looking skeptically over her glasses. She didn't give me time to answer. She was obviously adept at disappointment. "Are you here for the board meeting? Is that it?" I nodded. "Then follow me." She turned and walked down a hallway with fading pictures of men in thin or bow ties and glasses that went out of style years ago. She ushered me into the boardroom and shut the door behind her.

The man with the bonsai was at the head of the table; I assumed he was the board president. I cleared my throat. Nothing. He wrote something on a manila envelope. He had terrible handwriting; more like cuneiform than something legible. "Hello?" I offered.

He held up a finger that was either a sign he wanted me to wait or he was exercising his index finger. Other than the table, the mismatched chairs with duct tape patches and the odd flag, there was nothing else in the room, except a sour-smelling trash can filled with greasy lunch bags and crushed store-brand diet cola cans.

After five minutes and three reps of finger exercises, I decided to find the can. I went to the door, painted two shades of blue and discovered a shortage of doorknobs.

"Excuse me, the door is locked. I mean, there's no knob." This time, nothing. He just stared at his envelope with his pen leaking between his teeth.

I pulled out my cell phone. No bars. These old buildings are coverage vacuums. I sat back down just in time for the door to open briefly and shut faster.

The door opened and a thin man in a dark blue suit with a salmon-colored tie came in. He was tanned and looked confused. He walked to the table and held out his manicured fingers. "I'm Richard. I'm here for the board meeting." His voice was like an asthmatic wheeze. But it was nothing compared to the sound of the door closing.

He walked to the head of the table, leading with his outstretched hand. "Hi, I'm Richard." The bonsai man, dripping blue drool, ignored him as well. "I'm here for the board meeting," he spoke in a loud and deliberate voice as if the man was deaf instead of rude. Nothing.

"What's with him?" Richard asked, walking back to my side of the table.

I shrugged. "Beats me. I've been here nearly ten minutes and I am not sure he knows I'm here."

"Well, I am too busy a man to waste my time where I am clearly not wanted." He walked to the door and stared at the space where the knob should have been.

"Oh, by the way, we're trapped."

"Trapped?" He walked to the door and pushed it in at least three different places to no avail. He slapped at the door with his palm. "Excuse me? Excuse me?"

"The door is locked."

Richard plopped down next to me and muttered something about killing Arthur.

"Who's Arthur?" I asked.

"My asshole attorney. He said it would be good for business if I joined a board to show I care about people."

"My asshole is named Ellie. DBA, my guilt-ridden wife. What's your business?"

He reached into his Brooks Brothers sports jacket, and took out an expensive business card with his name followed by a slew of initials.

"You're a financial advisor," I translated.

"I am an independent investment counsel to high net worth individuals," Richard said. It was a wonder he was able to sit with that broom shoved up his ass. He looked at my clothes, liked what he saw, and asked me if I considered who was minding my money while I was minding my business.

"Save it, I am in the business, too. Ad Aspira Funds."

"Ad Aspira," Richard said, jutting out his chin. "Impressive deal last year for Republic. Made a pretty penny, didn't we?"

I rolled up my shirtsleeve and displayed my Patek Philippe watch. "Did all right." Richard looked at his business card on the middle of the table, dangerously close to a puddle of what looked to be flat soda. He dropped his slender fingers on his card and slipped it back into his Coach wallet.

He looked at his watch (a Tissot) and asked, "If we are trapped we might as well get started. I was told that board meetings were less than an hour." The man with bonsai wiped the drool from his chin and on to his cheek as if he was on the warpath. He was not the least bit embarrassed or even aware we were watching him.

Luckily for me the door opened and Richard shut up. A large man, the color of coffee with two milks, stuck his bald head in the door and smiled broadly. He was wearing a dark fleece jacket with an odd sports logo on the chest. He smiled as if we were long lost friends picking him up at the airport. Without asking or warning, he wrapped his enormous arms around Richard and me.

Unfortunately for both of us, we did not have the chance to reach the door before it shut. Richard was the first to break free and threw himself against the door.

The large man looked at me. I decided to call him Omar, as in the tentmaker.

"We're trying to escape," I explained.

"Ah," he said with an accent that was brewed at either Cambridge or Oxford. I figured the logo on his jacket was for some English soccer team.

He walked over to the door and searched for the doorknob, first in the obvious locations and then in the less traditional places. When he turned around he did not seem to be upset. "My bad," he said, reinstalling the smile on his face. "No worries. I am sure this is a misunderstanding." He dropped himself down in my chair and intertwined his bratwurst-sized fingers. "So, am I late for the meeting?"

"The meeting?" Richard asked, his forehead plastered against the wall.

"The board meeting?" Omar asked, fishing a small piece of paper from his shirt pocket. "I've been invited to the join the Fundation board." He frowned. "Silly name, right? But anything for a good cause."

"You in the business?" I asked.

"In the business?" Omar asked.

"Of doing good?"

He looked perplexed but his smile never faded. "Do you mean non-profit? No, but I am in the business of doing good. Actually doing great! I'm a management consultant." He padded his chest and buttocks. "I'm sorry, but I gave my last business card to the lady out front. Do you have one?" He took my card and wrote his email address on the back. "It's the only way you can reach me. I never sit still." He pushed back on the table with his enormous hands and tilted the chair into a precarious position.

I waited for him to flip over backwards, figuring we could escape through the hole in the floor. But he perched like one of those circus elephants balancing on two legs. "It's all about performance," he said. "It isn't about how smart you are. Who you know. It is about what you do. And I'm the man who gets you from here to there. There are two options when you are in a race." Race? Who mentioned anything about a race?

"Let's say you have two race cars," he said. "They are neck and neck coming into the final turn. There are two choices, right? Most people think 'I'm in a turn, I better slow down.' But the true performer knows this is the time to hit the gas and wins the race. Two options; one winner."

"There's a third option," I said.

"There is? What is it?"

"I could crash into the wall."

Great guffaws roared out his stomach as if he were some ancient volcano spirit. "Crash into the wall, that's rich. I suppose that could happen, but I wouldn't be much of a consultant if I said that, right?"

"What if it doesn't work out?"

"What doesn't work out?"

"The plan. What if you tried your best and you still failed? I mean, you don't guarantee success, do you?"

"Guarantee success? Of course not. That would be like being able to predict the future. We couldn't do that on the best day, could we? I put my clients in the best position to succeed. What they do from that position is solely up to them."

"But you get paid either way, right?"

"Good advice costs money."

"So does bad advice."

He tilted his enormous head and I could hear his mammoth brain sloshing about. "Pardon?"

"He's making fun of you," Richard said.

"Easy tiger, I was just having fun. No offense meant."

The door opened again and a woman with hair the color of hay came blinking into the room like she had been locked in a closet for the past few years. Judging by the Saran-wrap quality of her skin and her mouth which seemed incapable of closing, she'd had "work" done.

She launched an outstretched arm as many professional women do. They are so eager to be taken seriously they transform themselves into something that would be most at home on stage with a horned helmet and a bronze bustier.

We didn't make her feel welcome as the three of us lunged towards the door before it shut. We bumped into each other, hands outstretched as the door quietly shut. Richard was blubbering and shot the woman an evil look, which she responded to by holding out her hand towards him.

"Beverly Robin: Katchen, Munson, Berwood, LLC," she introduced herself. Richard grabbed her hand and nearly pulled her over.

To her credit, Beverly did not notice Richard's angry face and withdrew three business cards and handed one to Richard and then one to Omar and finally one to me. "Commercial real estate law."

She blinked at us, surprised that no one was shaking her hand or reading her card. She took a deep breath and composed herself. She sat down next to Richard and began to speak even though it was obvious he was in the midst of a breakdown.

She spoke quickly, like an enthusiastic ten-year-old. "So are you on the board, too? How long have you been on the board? Is it satisfying? I have to admit, I have never heard of this charity. I am on the Symphony auxiliary board, too. You wouldn't believe the hoops I had to jump through to get on that board. But you know, it was well worth it. I mean, it's for a good cause. Lots of business contacts and classical music. Two passions of mine. And with all my work at the firm and symphony, you would think I wouldn't be able to take on anything else. Especially for practical jokes."

She leaned over and whispered to Richard, but loud enough for all to hear. "I am not even sure there is any public good in funding practical jokes. I for one would like to see their IRS non-profit determination letter before I agree to anything. Can't be too careful, can you? Not that I am implying you're not careful. You are all successful men so I am sure you must have checked this out before you joined. That's good enough for me." She let out a short, high pitched giggle that she quickly stifled.

She took a long and overdue exhalation, tapped her long fingers on the table. "So when do we get started? I am ready, eager and have a very important meeting at 2:00 pm."

Richard moaned, "We can't leave."

"I don't understand. Why can't we leave?"

"Can't. Locked. No doorknob," Richard said.

She looked at Omar who said, "Afraid so."

She looked at me. I shrugged and nodded. "For how long?"

"As long as he wants us to stay," I said, pointing to the man with the Bonsai. He was looking for something under the table. He surfaced, muttered something to himself and then ducked under again.

"Excuse me," Beverly said, "Perhaps this is the wrong board for me. I would be happy to make a contribution." She reached into her briefcase and took out a checkbook and a gold pen. "Would five hundred do? Or even two-fifty?"

The man with the bonsai didn't say anything. He smiled as if he was remembering a joke someone had told him years ago that he wasn't sure he got.

We sat in silence, waiting for something to happen. For him to say something. For the door to open. There was only the sound of wheezing radiators and the disembodied voices below us.

Richard was shaking his cell phone, trying to get a signal. He had a difficult time sitting still; he fidgeted in his chair as if something was about to fall on him. Omar was leaning back in his chair with his big hands thrust into the pockets. He puffed out his cheeks like a beached whale. Beverly looked around, smiling in every direction. She would get up every so often, walk in a circle around the table and sit back down.

If this was supposed to be a redeeming experience, it was just what I expected. Who was I kidding, even if I gave a damn, what would I accomplish with my work for the foundation? One, maybe two people, could play a joke on someone else. At most maybe five people's lives would be changed for maybe a half an hour. They would laugh hard, then less hard and then not at all. Their lives would go on their own miserable way. I looked at my fellow inmates and tried to guess what brought them here.

Richard was in despair, perhaps wondering if this was some sort of punishment for his selfishness. He was probably the first one in his family to achieve wealth, and was the least charitable. His parents probably tithed and there was a jar in the kitchen in which one out of every ten dollars went for what he could only see as God's bribes. He probably blamed everything on that jar; his uncomfortable bed, his pants with holes in the knees and the taunts of the boys at school who asked him if he owned a sweater that fit. It took years to wash the smell of cabbage out of his skin. Richard had nothing to be ashamed of, but couldn't convince himself of that. He rested his head on his french cuffs and sighed, wondering what more was wanted of him.

On the other hand, Omar had grown up wealthy, the child of a Pakistani doctor. He lived in a wealthy suburb, surrounded by wealthy people. Hard work was their ethic. On Saturday nights relatives and neighbors came over for coffee and sweets and compared how far each of them had come. Charity was reserved for poor cousins overseas who ate the dirt they slept on. They knew real poverty and nothing America belched up could match it. Omar adopted his parents' aversion to helping the lazy instead of the truly desperate. Unless they have some sort of flesh-eating disease, there was nothing to discuss.

And Beverly, what did she care about except what others thought? It was impossible for me to tell what her childhood had been like. It was whatever was acceptable to others. If aestheticism was de rigueur she would have dressed herself in rags and eaten cat food. She was a cipher to herself. But one day with hard work and absolute compliance, she would be one of those who would tell people what to care about. And it wouldn't be anything sad.

We didn't notice when the door opened and our bald warden walked in and shut the door. She distributed the agenda comprised of four items: Introductions, Decision Items, Old Business and New Business.

We waited for the man with the bonsai to speak, if nothing else to introduce himself. But he seemed uninterested in the proceedings, barely looking at the paper that his bald helper placed in front of him.

"We have a light agenda today so we will skip the introductions," the bald woman said.

"We've had the opportunity to get to know each other," Richard said, sounding like a guitar string being wound too tightly. "But we don't know who he is or even who you are."

"His name is unimportant. Can we get to work?"

Richard pouted and shrugged. Omar nodded amicably and I said,

"Please." Beverly went with the consensus.

"Fine," she lifted her glasses to her forehead and held a paper closely to her eyes as if she was having trouble reading the print. "We can only fund one project and have two finalists. Candidate one is the president of a colon cancer foundation. She lost her mother and older sister to colon cancer. Now she is thirty-seven with two children, twelve and ten. Oh, and she is happily married. The proposal is to give her colon cancer with six months to live while she desperately fundraises for an experimental treatment that won't work.

"The other candidate is a six-year-old girl who is on a picnic with her parents. It is the first beautiful day of the year and it has been a difficult year with the single father losing his job and the older sister hospitalized for asthma. But the father has found a new job and the sister is healthy enough to go out. It seems that they have finally turned the corner. We propose a ball tossed into the parking lot, the girl runs after it and is struck and killed by a SUV driven by a teenager learning to drive. Should we take a vote or do you want to discuss it first?"

"These are horrible," Omar said, with a look of revulsion on his face.

"Horrible. Just horrible," Beverly said.

"You really want us to decide between killing a mother or a daughter?" Richard said, finding a reservoir of moral indignation.

"Then we are going to be here for a while," the bald woman said.

"This isn't what we signed up for," Richard spluttered.

"I guess the joke is on you," the bald woman said with not the tiniest bit of irony. But the man with the bonsai smiled wanly with blue teeth.

I waited for the revulsion to build. Any normal person would refuse to even consider it. I should be nauseated. I should be incensed. I wasn't. I tried to imagine the faces of the woman and the girl, but they were simply blurred like suspects on "Cops." I should have cared. I didn't. I couldn't.

I looked over at the man with the bonsai. His eyes were tightly closed as if he was screening out a thousand voices. He opened his right eye and stared at me with a look of kinship and desperation.

"Let's go with the mother," I said. The others stared at me as if I had a repulsive hair lip.

"You're kidding," Richard said, noticeably sweating.

You could watch the gears in Omar's head as he fought to find something positive about my vote. "Now you are the one joking."

"No, I'm not. The mother dying is funnier."

"How can you say that?" Beverly asked. She was whiter than the paper she fanned herself with.

"Easy," I said, "she is fighting colon cancer and gets colon cancer. It's ironic."

"It's sick," Richard said and Beverly nodded.

"Look, I am not saying it is 'ha-ha' funny. All I am saying is that it's funnier than a girl getting hit by a car. That's what we are here to judge, right?"

"But you are killing a woman, a mother, a wife," Beverly blurted in quick succession.

"No, I'm not. I'm fulfilling my role as a board member."

"I absolutely refuse to participate in this awful, awful act." Richard got up and walked to the far side of the wall as if he wanted to be as far away from me as possible. Beverly got up and looked at Richard and me. Without waiting to see what Omar would do, she walked over to stand with Richard.

"I am sorry, mate, but you really are one sick fuck," Omar said, his brows were like thunderheads.

"Someone asked me my opinion and I gave it. I don't see why you are making a federal case out of it. If you three want to vote for the girl getting run over, that's fine with me. I don't care."

Richard, Omar and Beverly were appalled and refused to vote. I heard the sound of rustling behind me. The man with the bonsai was smiling. He straightened the papers in the manila file, left it at the head of the table and stood up. He walked with a slight limp, like his foot was asleep. He placed the bonsai in front of me and walked to the door, went through and left it open.

Waiting

> What the hell is a polished piece and why would I want to eat it?

It has the elegance of a fifty-year-old waiting room in a small-market Midwestern bus station. The benches are dark wood, carved in such a way as to lull one's buttocks asleep and yet be completely uncomfortable. The air in the room has been recycled for years and smells of sweat, old gum, and lint. The overhead pendant lights don't illuminate so much as serve as efficient grime-covered insect collectors. The walls are hues of white, ranging between beige, yellow, and filth.

Someone, many years ago, made an effort to brighten up the room with depictions of buses with stylized hoods advertising destinations that now have reduced or no bus service. One offers a bus with an impassive Indian head, advertising "Beautiful Sioux City" that someone had appended in ball-point pen, "Shit City."

A greasy water fountain hangs on one wall, with an empty cup dispenser next to it hanging precariously on a nail. Next to it, an old vending machine features stale potato chips, dusty chocolate bars, and an unfamiliar brand of mints and fruit drops. On the opposite wall is a wooden information rack, mostly empty except for the small pamphlets inviting the reader to accept Jesus as his lord and savior and an advertisement for the Doll-of-the-Month Club that promises "flesh-like finish." Finally, on the fourth wall is the door with "To Bu s s" painted on the stippled amber glass window.

Who is in the room? It is difficult to tell. Some people are fully present with all features and details of boredom drawn on their faces. Others are more ideas than anything else; faceless shadows who lean against the wall with spectral bodies. And some are somewhere in between, with looks of disgust, depression, or mindless enthusiasm. If you ask them what they are thinking they will tell you in intricate detail. If you ask them for their biography, they will stutter and seem to be making it up as they spoke.

One of the more fully drawn people, a man in his late fifties, who would remind you of an elf if an elf wore red flannel and brown corduroy, reaches under the bench for a two-quart-sized thermos filled with ice cubes, a two-liter bottle of Diet Mt. Chill, and a large plastic mug from Casey's General Store. He pours a good fourteen ounces of pop into the mug, fishes out five ice cubes from the thermos, and drops them in; they hiss in protest. "It is most inconvenient," he says with a drawl, the origin of which is located somewhere north of Kentucky but south of Carbondale. He looks around and sees no one paying much attention to his opinion. "Most inconvenient, it you ask me."

The man next to him, and he appears to be male based on his outline, groaned. He is at least six-foot three with strong arms and legs. The silhouette cast by his hair is full and luxurious, the type you would love to run your fingers through. The only thing missing is any sort of facial features. His legs stretch out and cross, echoing his arms' impatience.

He exhales in exasperation and says to no one in particular, "What's that? Most inconvenient? Since when do you use terms like 'most inconvenient?' You sound like a Southern lady with a painful secret. You know, the one in which she claims she was raped by a family friend? That secret. The one she shares with everyone while asking you to keep it to yourself. Is that what you are implying? Some sort of secret in your past? You wish." Even though he didn't have a mouth, you can feel the sneer.

Our friend the elf shrugs and takes a healthy pull on his straw. "All I'm saying is that I am getting tired of waiting. Waiting and never knowing when or if I will be called." His accent comes down out of the hills and finds its way to mid-state Illinois, somewhere near Bloomington.

"Then fucking say so. Don't go all Glass Menagerie on me."

"Excuse me if I prefer to be a bit more courteous. Most inconvenient," he says, staring into the handsome man's face where the eyes should be. He is pretty sure he is being glowered at.

"If you don't like it, then just go. There's the door," the indefinite man, waving his indistinct fingers in the direction of the door, says. "It's not locked."

"Why don't you go?" the elf says, his voice shaking, which he hoped would be interpreted as anger and not as fear. He hadn't liked the faceless man from the moment he showed up almost a week ago. When he first appeared, he was all height and attitude—seventy some inches of arrogance and privilege.

The elf had seen his type before. They materialize suddenly and gradually become more defined, handsome, and aloof until you couldn't look at them without feeling self-conscious. Soon no one was speaking in the waiting room. You could feel the relief when they left and people could make small talk again.

They were always successful, these handsome faceless ones. They were lawyers, doctors, military heroes and, if you looked closely, their feet never touched the ground. Our elf has been in the waiting room long enough to know there is always an inch or two between the bottom of their very expensive Italian loafers and the grimy linoleum floor. It wasn't fair. They showed up out of nowhere with nothing but an outline. They talked to no one, except to snort when someone expressed frustration or sadness. They grew more handsome and cocky and then they were gone. Out the door with purpose and direction.

The handsome man, who is developing thick, rich, red curly hair, walks to the door and grasps it with the profile of a palm. The door slides open as if relieved. "See? It's not locked. You can leave at any time. All of you can leave at any time. But what do you do? You sit in here and wait. For what? Him? Have you seen this guy? Have you talked to him? No. For whatever reason, you think he's in charge. That's the most pathetic thing I have ever heard." He slams the door shut; it's a miracle the glass doesn't break. He floats over to the bench and throws himself down into an angry, ambivalent pile. The elf notices almond-shaped brown eyes beginning to appear in the middle of the man's face.

Having nothing else to do, the elf takes a long drink. The pop tastes like dried grass. He refills the mug with an amount equal to what he had just drunk. Holding up the bottle, he hopes it will be emptier. But he sees the line he had incised in the label with his thumb nail. He squints and no matter at what angle he holds the bottle, the Diet Mt. Chill dances in perfect unison with the line. How many years has he been drinking from this bottle? Two? Five? Forever? He can't remember a time when he didn't have the thermos, the mug and the two-liter bottle of Diet Mt. Chill.

One of the handsome faceless men had called him Mr. Chill. "How's it going, Mr. Chill? Been to the mountain lately?" He laughed and looked at the rest of the people, who would laugh politely for fear of being labeled next. At least the current handsome man doesn't call him Mr. Chill. He may be pathetic, but he wasn't Mr. Chill.

"I can't leave," the elf finally says. "I left once," he says to the small girl with dark brunette pigtails who sits next to him. She is wearing a pink dress with purple polka dots. She looks six, but the elf has known her for at least two years and she has yet to age.

"You left without being called?" she asks in a sing-song voice. The freckles on her nose gleamed innocently.

He nods.

"What's it like?"

"I wasn't out there too long. There's no point of going out if you don't know where you are going. So I came back in."

"He was scared shitless," the faceless handsome man says, sticking an invisible chin in the air.

"Why don't you leave?" the elf says. The little girl covers her ears. She hates when people argue. She doesn't like any feeling that isn't happy. She looks over at the teenage black boy leaning against the far corner. He pulled the hood of his orange sweatshirt over his face and all you could see is a straw that he has been chewing for days. He digs his hands into the pockets of his pants that are almost halfway down his hips. She doesn't like him. He uses lots of bad words and her mother told her to avoid boys like him.

"Why leave, when I am going to be called at any moment?" the faceless man said. "I am not long for this room. All he needs to do is fill in my eyes, nose, and mouth and I am out of here. And all of you will be still here, waiting. And that's exactly what you will be doing, waiting. Waiting. Waiting forever."

"Don't listen to him," the elf says to the little girl. "You'll get out of here soon. Want some?" he asks, holding up the straw for her to take a sip.

She shakes her head rapidly so that the little cubes on her pigtail hair holders clink like castanets. Her mother warned her about older men offering her drinks, too. "No, I don't think I will leave anytime soon. What does he know about me? That we were friends in first grade. In his mind, we were boyfriend and girlfriend. In first grade? And if I hadn't moved to Illinois, we would have fallen in love, gotten married, and lived happily ever after." She dangles her hands, limp at the wrists, over her head in a sarcastic gesture well beyond her years. "That's what he thinks. If my dad hadn't gotten a job in Wheaton, he would have been happy instead of stuck with what-could-have-beens.

"There's not much you can do with that. A girl you knew thirty-eight years ago for maybe six months? Anything more than that and they'll accuse you of overreaching. You know how much he hates that. So he needs more details before I go anywhere. But he's has nothing besides my hair, freckles, and dress. He doesn't even know what color my eyes are," she says as her irises went from blue to brown to green back to blue in rapid succession. "Looks like I am stuck here for a long time. Maybe he'll lose interest in me," she says, not believing a word.

"Heck," the elf says, "I would be glad if he would give me a name. I don't know if I'm Irish or German or what. I don't even know how old I am. I guess I am between fifty and sixty. Judging by my clothes and my bottle of Diet Mt. Chill, I am not a rich man. I don't think I am all that smart either. I seem nice enough, but I am not sure if I am or if I am the sort of man you would least expect to be an axe murderer until you look under my bedroom's floor boards. I would hate to think that." He shudders and tries to resist the temptation to drink, but he is always thirsty when he is uncomfortable. He swallows half the mug, grimaces, adds a few more ice cubes and pours in some more pop. The level in the bottle unmercifully stays the same.

"The only thing you could do is bore somebody to death," the handsome man says. "Look at me, he didn't give me a name, but I'm calling myself Chris. Christopher Allen Patterson." He looks at the elf and the girl with irisless eyes. "Junior," he adds, with an empty chin raised in the air. "He can call me anything he wants, but I know who I am. That's why he's so afraid of me, because he knows he can't control me. He's more afraid of me than Chuckles over there," he said, pointing with the outline of a hand toward the young black man in the corner.

"Mutherfucka," the boy says through his straw.

"God help us if he ever gets out. The streets will be littered with stereotypes. I really don't know why he thinks he can get away with him. The closest he ever came to a gangbanger is watching *The Wire*. Not much for verite, if you ask me."

"Sheeeet," the black boy says, crossing his arms in something that is supposed to be gang sign but looks more like a wind-blown television antenna.

The door opens; an elderly black couple walks in. They are dressed modestly, she in a blue cloth coat buttoned to her neck and he in a tan sport coat with a yellow shirt, brown tie, and navy blue pants. He wears a plaid stingy-brimmed fedora, which he immediately takes off and kneads in his hands, with a large gold Masonic ring on his right ring finger. They survey the room, looking slowly at the elf and the small girl on one bench, the faceless handsome man sprawled out on another and the angry black boy in the corner. He looks up at them and exhales loudly as if he had been punctured. They stand near him, but not too close. He doesn't acknowledge them; but just stares straight ahead, chewing his straw that waves like a conductor's baton.

"Jesus, we're going to be knee-deep in clichés in a matter of minutes," Christopher Junior says.

The elf looks at the elderly black couple. They are obviously familiar with suffering and bear it with a simple dignity. He tried dignity once, but it felt like pants that were two sizes too small. He straightens his spine and pulls his hips forward. He interlaces his fingers behind his back in a pose that speaks of wisdom and perseverance. He holds his chin up and purses his lips. He wanders about the waiting room as if considering the plights of his compatriots and tries to comfort them by example. The handsome faceless man of the moment—a brunette—sniffs with lipless mouth. "What's-a matter? You look like you gotta take a dump." Every bone in the elf's body crumbles like a house of cards in a stiff breeze.

The black couple huddles together, speaking in quiet tones. They look at the bench on which the faceless man smirks without a mouth. There is plenty of room for them, but they prefer to stand. The older man begins to cough and holds up a handkerchief dotted with blood. When he coughs, his whole body shakes as if it is about to fall apart. His wife rests her hand on his shoulders, holding him together.

"Oh, for Christ's sake!" the faceless man says, getting up. "Sit down, already. I'm sure you'll lose a lung soon." He walks over to the vending machine and stares into it. "Will you look at this crap? Stale pretzels, crushed cookies, and candy from a company I never heard of. You know what they say Hemingway had in his waiting room? Bourbon and steaks this thick." He approximates the width of the steaks with fingerless hands. "They say Michael Chabon has a deli platter flown in fresh daily from Zabar's. What do we get?" he asks, peering through the dusty glass that is nearly as transparent as he. "Fox's Polished Pieces. What the hell is a polished piece and why would I want to eat it?" The room is silent except for the susurrations of the elf's soda and the old black man's quiet hacking.

The waiting-room door's handle turns and the door slowly opens but no one enters. All stare in anticipation that they will be called. But the door just stays open. There is a strange noise on the other side: thump, thump, scrape, groan, thump, thump, scrape, groan. Two small rubber tips on the bottom of canes appear. And then two hands attached to short arms emerging from a blue blazer's sleeve. And finally a man no taller than four-feet-nine inches with an enormous white beard and pompadour struggles into view. He smiles at everyone and wishes them a good morning in a cheerful loud voice. He has metal braces on his legs and has a strange mode of propelling himself, placing one cane forward and then the other, pulling his lifeless legs forward, groaning at the end by way of punctuation.

"Oh, God, not another dwarf!" the faceless handsome man, who now has nostrils to flare, says. "What's with him and dwarves? He looks at the open door. "It is beyond me why we wait to be rescued by an obvious hack. Let's face it. In his hands, we're better ideas than people."

The pop sizzles as the elf drops in fresh ice cubes.

Acknowledgments

I would like to acknowledge the following people, without whom all of this would be merely a bad head day. Maud and Lila, who have suffered through being my daughters and all that entails. Leslie Cleaver, who dusts the cobwebs away and has the world's bawdiest laugh. Andy Finkle, the world's greatest artist and generous friend. Tim Brandhorst of Aquitaine Media for not knowing any better. Richard Friedman, for his red pen and friendship. And family and friends too numerous to mention, but not to appreciate. Finally, for Muddles, Lola and Joey, for injecting just the right amount of insanity into my life.